Meg's Men

Meg's Men

ROBERTA BEST

Published by Jackson Publishing

A CIP catalogue record for this book is available from the British Library.

ISBN 978-1-9196452-1-6

Book layout and cover design by Clare Brayshaw

Cover   92709177 © Kiosea39 | Dreamstime.com
         136762537 © Mia Stendal | Dreamstime.com

Prepared and printed by:

York Publishing Services Ltd
64 Hallfield Road
Layerthorpe
York YO31 7ZQ

Tel: 01904 431213

Website: www.yps-publishing.co.uk

Chapter 1

THE dark winter days were short, the house a prison. I must get out, she thought, or go quietly mad. Charles would accept her being mad, it would be another of the crosses he would have to bear along his path of life.

"Perhaps I shall go to evening classes again." Charles looked up, alarm flitted across his furrowed brow.

"Not be here in the evenings?" He was really worried now. He eyed her over the top of his spectacles.

"It would only be one evening a week."

"Don't you enjoy my company in the evenings?" He really was rather pathetic.

You bore me silly, she wanted to scream at him but tamped down the idea.

"Of course dear, it's lovely just the two of us here."

"Well then?"

"Oh, I thought it might be nice to go out, meet people you know." Charles patently did not know.

"Hmm, well I shall be late." Didn't he say that every day and was he ever late?

Unthinkable.

"Goodbye dear, until six." A brief brushing of cheeks, a momentary pecking of the empty air and he was gone.

Hells teeth, thought Meg. What have I done to deserve this? She mechanically worked her way through the household routine. Washing, cleaning, the beds.

Charles' bed, smooth, barely ruffled, another disciplined night obviously. Her own bed looked as though she had fought off an entire rugby team. God, I wouldn't fight them, they would be very welcome. She tried to remember if there were thirteen or fifteen in a team.

Jane and Barbara would be arriving soon, it was Meg's turn to be hostess for their Tuesday coffee morning. A quick snort of brandy before they arrived and perhaps the morning would not be so abrasive.

Meg settled down with a large double and the previous evenings paper. 'Local farmer weds insurance clerk, she read. Good for him. 'Council in deadlock over new road'. 'School,' none of it held any interest for her. She turned to the personal column, sometimes good for a giggle. Nothing. An advert for a marriage bureau. How very old fashioned. Meg thought everyone looked for partners on the internet these days. Perhaps there were still people who were not computer savvy or liked this way of contact. It would certainly suit her, she thought. The only times she had used the computer, which sat in the corner of the living room Charles always knew. Flitting through a page of recipes and finding nothing which appealed she had consigned her search to the bin in the corner of the device. Charles had been able to retrieve her searches and asked why she didn't want the recipes. After that she rarely consulted the internet. This advert seemed a good way to avoid arousing Charles' interest. There was a number given to ring. A sudden impulse made her want to ring and ask for details. But with a start she realised it was time for the girls to arrive.

Girls, she thought cynically, there's not one of us will see forty again. Just time for a quick scrub at her teeth to get rid of the brandy smell and the doorbell was chiming. Throughout the morning, listening with half an ear to her friends idle prattling, Meg was speculating about the marriage bureau. After the second cup of coffee she had definitely decided to ring the number. Once the decision was made she could not get rid of the others quickly enough. The number rang out for some time before a sugary voice answered.

"Hilary Hall Bureau, can I help you?"

"It's about your advert in the evening paper. I wondered if you.. that is I wanted.. can I ask." Meg struggled in a way that was entirely foreign to her.

"Perhaps if I were to give you some details you could then ask me any questions," said the silken voice.

"Yes, please," replied Meg feebly.

"We try to maintain complete anonymity for our lady clients, until they are sure they would really like to meet the gentleman. Therefore we would ask that you only put a phone number on your first letter and you can then make arrangements to meet if you have something in common. I will send you a list of clients most suited to you when you have told me a little about yourself. The fees are three hundred pounds for the first five introductions. A further two hundred is payable if marriage results from one of our introductions. Three hundred sounded a bit steep but, oh sod it, it might be fun.

Meg gabbled off a lot of nonsensical rubbish about herself, exchanged addresses with sugary voice and rang off, her head spinning. God, I'm a good liar, she thought, but what am I doing? I don't need to met a crowd of misfits. Why, I might be putting myself in danger. Heaven alone knew what might be the motives of men writing to such a place.

The morning post brought a fat envelope with her five introductions and a great deal of information about the best way to write a first letter. Also a wedge of recommendations and letters purporting to come from satisfied clients, now safely married off to each other.

"Anything interesting?" said Charles over the top of his newspaper.

"An invitation to a school reunion."

"A lot of paper for an invite."

"Yes, well there's a sort of information sheet with it, you know, what old girls are doing, that sort of thing. Rather like a school magazine."

"Hmm." Charles had lost interest and gone back to the editorial in The Telegraph. I'm sure he doesn't enjoy that paper, Meg thought, it must be too high- brow for him. She had always imagined him as an intellectual nonentity and yet he had done well at his job. Perhaps being manager of an insurance firm was what made him so dull. No, he had always been dull. She was sure he had been a dull baby and a boring school boy. He had probably taken refresher courses since then on how to maintain standards of boredom.

"Well, goodbye dear, mustn't be late." Not a chance.

"Goodbye, until six." The token air kissing routine and he was gone, no doubt to bore the office crowd. Meg met some of his colleagues at the Christmas parties, they might all have been brothers and sisters of Charles. Mirror images.

Chapter 2

MEG took out her list of introductions again. M36 Bachelor, thirty-eight, five feet ten. Interests include church music and collecting butterflies. Meg had a mental image of herself romping over the countryside with a butterfly net, pursued by a cleric in a cassock.

P495.Divorcee, fifty, six feet. Interested in swimming, golf and brass rubbing. S75. Thirty-eight, five eleven. A keen gardener and dog lover. Meg didn't think the two were compatible, unless the dog was trained to dig up other peoples lawns and to pee on strangers' flowers.

G84.Bachelor, forty-three, six feet. Interests were travel and embroidery. Jesus, Meg thought.

C33.Bachelor. Forty-five five feet (there was a blur on the paper and this candidate could have been anywhere between five nothing and five eleven.) What on earth did height matter anyway, she thought. Surely it would be more to the point to put down their occupations. That would be a starting point for a first letter, what do you do? Besides writing to marriage bureaux?

Charles returned home at six, as predictable as ever. He carried a bulging briefcase. Obviously a working weekend, noted Meg. She wondered how to fill her Sunday while Charles shuffled his papers round the dining-room table.

"Had a good day?" he asked. Charles' idea of a good day was one in which nothing out of the ordinary happened. He preferred no ripples on the surface of his mill pond.

"Not really. There was an accident outside Marks and Spencers, an old man was knocked down." There had been no accident, it was all a figment of her imagination. Meg was a pathological liar. Faced with the truth or a falsehood Meg always chose the lie. It was something over which she had little control. She thought it gave her a more interesting image, a more romantic air. Often; through firmly entrenched habit; she would lie when there was no advantage to be gained.

"The police have been here this afternoon to take a statement, there were two of them," she added, warming to her theme.

"Was he badly hurt?" She toyed with the idea of killing off the fictitious victim.

"Taken to hospital," she called as she went into the kitchen, suddenly tiring of the game.

"Benson got his monthly returns in a pickle again. I've brought them home to see if I can help him. He ought to retire, he's getting past it." Charles the Cavalry to the rescue again.

"Poor old soul," Meg murmured, sympathetic in her new role as champion of downtrodden and knocked- down old men.

The evening meal was soon over and Charles was buried in the papers he had brought home. A quick scurry round restoring order and Meg was ready for her papers.

Meg read through the list again. Not a very dynamic bunch. She thought of the brief resume of herself that she had sent off with her cheque, it must read just like this. I'll write to them all, she decided yes, even the embroiderer. She sat at the dining-room table and wondered what to say.

Better to make it as light-hearted as possible, she didn't suppose anyone would want to know an old sober side. If they didn't like her sense of humour then they wouldn't bother contacting her and there would be nothing lost.

In the end Meg wrote exactly the same letter to them all. She wondered what the reference numbers meant but was unable to hazard a guess so addressed them by their numbers.

The instructions were to put the number in the top corner and leave the front blank. The bureau would put the different addresses on the envelopes. All her envelopes were put into one large one and addressed to the Hilary Hall Bureau. Meg posted it on Wednesday afternoon and was prepared for a long wait before she had an answer. It crossed her mind that none of the people really existed and that it was a huge confidence trick to squeeze money out of gullible fools. The rest of the week was taken up with the usual round of frivolous social contacts, shopping and household routines.

On Friday evening the phone rang as they were finishing their meal. Charles never answered the ring if Meg were about. He always assumed it was for her and was completely incurious about any calls unless they concerned him personally. Charles retired behind his newspaper and left Meg to answer the call. Meg had not thought she could have such a rapid response to her letters and was taken aback and rather panic stricken to hear a pleasant male voice.

"Is that Lyz?" She remembered with a jolt that she had put her middle name on the bureau form.

The voice had the suggestion of a west country accent. "I had your letter today and found it very amusing." A good start.

Meg clutched the phone tightly to quell the rising panic in her throat, she found the voice warm and exciting in a quite disturbing way. Having no way of knowing which of the men she was speaking to, she wondered how to broach the topic without it being too obvious that he was only one of many. She was also uncomfortably aware of Charles, hidden behind his paper. Any out of the way remark might raise his interest.

"By the way," said the voice, as though reading her thoughts "I'm G 84. G is for Gordon." Meg instantly realised how the filing system worked. The initial was for the clients' first name. She frantically tried to recall whether this was the guy with the butterfly net or the dog lover. Neither apparently.

"You recall that I'm interested in travel and embroidery." He could also read minds over the phone.

"Yes of course, I remember."

"I was wondering if we could meet, a drink perhaps or a meal?"

"Yes. I would like that."

"I see from your phone number that you live in Castlebridge." Bright spark. Meg was becoming aware that Charles had stopped rustling the paper. She smiled at him, gave a vague shrug and moved into the kitchen. Charles smiled back. Meg turned her attention back to the phone.

Chapter 3

"AS I'm in Wasterburn, perhaps we could meet at Sandford." This was a little market town mid-way between Castlebridge and Wasterburn and Meg felt it unlikely that anyone would know her there.

"Yes that would be good. I do have a car."

"I'm afraid Wednesday is my only free day, is that alright?"

"Wednesday is fine. What time?"

"If you could make it eleven we might have a drink and a chat before we had a spot of lunch. Meg agreed to this , thinking lunch sounded excellent.

"Wednesday then. Do you know the Hare and Hounds, the pub in the market."

"Yes, fine I know it." How repetitive her conversation must sound she thought. Gordon seemed not to notice and said goodbye.

"Goodbye," she almost bit off her tongue as she stopped herself uttering his name.

"Assignations?" Charles wandered in the kitchen looking for coffee.

"Hardly, Charles. Just arranging to meet one of the girls for coffee. She is trying to get several of our class together before the school meeting. Sandford is a mid point for most of us, we don't any of us seemed to have moved very far. He went back to the other room and turned on the television. It would be Panorama. Meg shut herself in the kitchen while Charles watched his programme. Gordon, she rolled the name round her tongue, a good solid ring to it. A manly name. He had forgotten to say how she would recognise him, never mind there would not be dozens of men waiting outside the pub.Meg remembered the Hare and Hounds as a rather scruffy pub tucked away between Barclays bank and the scout shop. Her thoughts occupied her so exclusively that she didn't hear the phone ringing again.

"Meg," shouted Charles irritably. Lazy devil, the phone is only a few yards from you she thought.

"Coming dear," her hands were still wet as she picked up the receiver.

"Is Lyz there please?" A rather breathless voice as though he could not get the words out quickly enough.

"Yes, this is .." she coughed with the sudden realisation that Panorama might not be totally absorbing. "This is she, who is speaking please?"

"You don't know me but you wrote me a letter. That sounds silly. What I meant was, that I'm Charles." Heaven help us, one Charles was enough.

"I'm the C 33 you wrote to." She remembered the bachelor who might well turn out to be quassimodo.

"How tall are you?" she said rather rudely

"I'm five ten." said a rather surprised voice. "Does it matter a lot?"

"Not really."

"I live in Chester, is it rather far for you do you think?"

"Rather far?" repeated Meg. Whatever does he mean, he surely doesn't want me to walk the forty odd miles to Chester.

"Well, it's just that I don't drive and the trains are rather awkward. I had hoped you could come over here. You did say you had a car." Cheeky sod, he sounded the way Charles did when he wasn't getting his own way. Whiney and plaintive. Maybe all Charles' were alike.

"I expect I could. When?"

"I only thought it might be easier." For you no doubt. Meg said nothing. "You see I have a business and only close for a few hours in the middle of the day."

"Which day would be best then?" I must sound terribly pushy, she thought.

"Thursday? I could meet you about one o'clock. Under the clock at the station?"

"I'll be there. Oh, how will I know you?" She was conscious that Charles was looking at her, his programme must be dull.

"You can't miss me," she shouted gaily down the phone. "I haven't changed at all."

"Another one for school reunion?"

"Charlotte, Charlotte Peters, you must have heard me mention her." Since Meg had only invented her that moment it wasn't very likely.

"Er, hmm, but why did you ask how tall she is? It sounded terribly rude."

No, old Charlie won't mind. It was all a bit of a joke at school. She was such a bean pole."

"And how tall is she?"

"Five ten."

"That's not too unusual."

"Well, she was always so thin at school she must have looked taller."

Meg was suddenly bored with the turn the conversation had taken. She muttered about finishing the washing up and went back to the kitchen after turning the ten o'clock news on for Charles. As entertainment the news was a non starter for Meg, she preferred to make up her own news.

Saturday was another routine for Charles. He would set off for the library at ten-thirty, take a leisurely walk around the town if the weather was not too bad and call at the club for a drink and a chat with friends. This Saturday he announced that he would have a hair cut but would be back for lunch at the usual time.

"Yes dear." She was hardly listening, willing him out of the house before the phone rang again. If Gordon and Charles had their letters so quickly, then it was quite on the cards that the other three men might ring her soon.

Charles took an irritatingly long time to find his library books, he had his coat on and then decided to take it off again. Oh go on, go on, she wanted to yell at him. He decided that it was cold enough for his heavy coat. He took years finding it but at last came downstairs wearing it. At last he was gone. Meg poured a large brandy and willed the phone to ring. The house was very quiet.

Chapter 4

ALTHOUGH she was listening for the phone and expecting it to ring, she none-the -less started guiltily when the bell rang out.

"It's Charles," it didn't sound like him, she realised her mistake when the voice went on. "You remember, I rang you last evening." Oh Lord, that Charles. "It just seemed confusing, about us meeting I mean."

"Of course. If I carry a green umbrella and wear a green coat then you will be able to find me won't you?"

"Yes, I expect so. What if there's more than one woman in green?" Meg wondered if someone as anxious as this ought to be walking the streets at all. He obviously believed in meeting troubles more than half way.

"Please don't worry so Charles, I'll find you."

"Would it be best to go for a meal do you think or not? What do you think Lyz?"

"We'll talk about that when we meet shall we?"

"Yes but, it would have been, I would have liked to get it all straight beforehand." Oh dear, we might all be run over by a bus before then she thought.

"Until Thursday," she said firmly and rang off before he could raise any more difficulties. She had hardly replaced the receiver when the phone rang again.

"Hello. I may speak please to Lyz?" There was a question and a foreign intonation to the voice. Meg introduced herself and waited. "My name is Sven and I have a letter from you." The only 'S' in the introductions was the gardener cum dog lover.

"Do you like dogs," he said, confirming that she had the right man.

"Love them. I had a beautiful labrador, but she died last month." She felt a genuine regret for this fictitious creature.

"Oh dear that is so sad, always a little part of you dies when they go." Meg felt her eyes go swimmy at the thought of her ghostly pet and at the same time warmed to this sentimental man.

"Very much I would like to meet you." Very much I would like to meet you, she thought but said nothing.

"Perhaps this weekend you are busy." Again the question in the voice.

"Yes, I am rather but Sunday afternoon I'll be free." She had suddenly remembered the bulging brief case Charles had brought home.

"I live only in Sandford and would be pleased to come to Castlebridge." No ruddy fear, thought Meg, this is too small a town to be seen meeting a man. There would be sure to be all the world and his wife waiting about on a Sunday afternoon for someone to gossip about.

"Actually, I shall be in Sandford on Sunday, visiting an aunt," she added. Meg had never had an aunt, but she felt sure that if she had then the aunt would live in Sandford, it was rather 'genteel'.

"That is nice, then we can meet. I know a cafe, it is open on Sundays."

"I would like that, it will have to be after four, you know my aunt"

"Shall we say quarter past four in the Linden Tree cafe, do you know it?" Meg agreed that she knew it and rang off feeling quite dizzy. How could she have thought a few days ago that life was dull. There was all this untapped excitement waiting to be reached out for. That sorted out Sunday, Wednesday and Thursday. She was well content with the response to her letters and happily set about preparing lunch. She felt quite warm toward Charles and decided to do his favourite pudding although it was rather intricate and she didn't much care for it herself. Charles was delighted and took little persuading to eat her share. He came out to the garden later and helped tie up some late chrysanthemums beaten down by the rain. The evening was one of the longest Meg remembered. Charles seemed absorbed by his crosswords and the mediocre television programmes. There was an excitement within Meg which kept rising up into her throat and threatening to bubble forth in a wild laugh. I wonder what he would do if I were to take off my clothes and lie on the hearth rug. He would probably turn the TV onto B.B C.2 and step over me to do so she thought. She had a large double brandy and went to bed early. Charles raised an eyebrow as she poured the drink, declined one for himself and turned the programme to B.B.C 2.

Meg dressed in her new green coat and walked serenely to church on Charles' arm next morning.

She nodded gently at the parish pussies, smiled impishly at the choirboys and shook hands elegantly with the vicar, whilst murmuring encouragingly about his sermon.

"A snack lunch?" asked Charles. "I really must get on with those papers for old Benson."

She cleared the lunch things, left their evening meal all prepared and looked in on Charles where he sat at the table happily sifting and shuffling reams of papers.

"Shan't be long, just going for a spin, I don't want to disturb you. The house will be quieter if I'm not pottering about," she justified herself.

Charles nodded absently and glanced vaguely over the top of his glasses. Meg had the idea that he sometimes wondered who she was when she spoke to him. The weather had turned about and a steady drizzle persisted as she drove to Sandford. The church clock showed just after four as she parked in the market square. Meg had forgotten her umbrella and was waiting for a break in the steady downpour, when the door of the Linden Tree cafe opened and a figure began waving frantically at her. Oh, no, she thought, not one of Charles' boring colleagues. The figure suddenly ran towards her brandishing a large umbrella.

"You must be Lyz?"

"That's right."

"Come, run with me and you will not be wet." They ran across the square, both clutching the brolly and laughing as they tried to avoid the puddles. They arrived at the cafe door, damp, out of breath and completely at ease with each other. Meg had met Sven.

Meg drove rather fast and aware that the evening meal would be late. Charles would not mind too much, although he would grumble from habit. Although she did not take this too seriously she had no wish to cross Charles unnecessarily. Despite her boredom and general feling of dissatisfaction with her life, she was well aware of which side her bread was buttered. It was a comfortable life, she had no money problems and Charles asked for very little from her. The least she could do would be to make sure things were running smoothly for him.

Chapter 5

THE meal was well under way before Charles appeared at the kitchen door and asked if she had enjoyed her spin out.

"It was lovely, I met a friend and we had tea in a cafe."

"I didn't have any tea," reproachfully.

"Never mind dear, you'll enjoy your dinner all the more."

"I suppose. I'll set the table for you. Would you like a sherry whilst we wait?" Meg felt she would rather have a large brandy, but accepted the sherry with a smile and a pretty 'thank you'. She really felt quite affectionate toward Charles and wondered if the sherry might be his way of softening her up, a prelude to one of his rare sexual advances.

Charles was very obvious and as predictable as ever. Meg lay there and imagined it was Sven making love to her. He would surely be a more imaginative lover. From the moment they had entered the cafe door, shaking the rain from their coat sleeves, there had been joy in the encounter. Sven did not sound so foreign as he had on the phone and he had a carefree, easy manner which made being with him a sheer delight. Meg was able to relax in his company in a way she had almost forgotten during her years with Charles.

He was broad with an open face, fair hair and the palest eyes Meg had ever seen. They gave him a rather vulnerable look, as though they would readily fill with tears when he was distressed.

Sven told Meg of his early years in Ostersund, of how they went to Ornskoldsvik for their holidays. The impossible Swedish names rolled off his tongue and to Meg they were as music.

The brief afternoon had flown away and they had parted regretfully but with a promise to meet again the following Friday when Sven had a day off from his job as a representative for a drugs firm. He had made even this humdrum occupation appear amusing. He had entertained her with funny stories of the different chemists he had to visit and the many old and odd characters he met in the medical profession. Some were so old fashioned he wondered if they had heard of penicillin. For her part Meg told of her childhood in the fishing village where she lived and her years as a boarder at the local grammar school in Wasterburn. Sven said he knew the school in Wasterburn and the girls all looked as though they were princesses who would know immediately if there was a pea under the mattress. Meg had laughed, said he was foolish and agreed to meet the following week. So relaxed had she been that she so far forgot herself as to say that she must go home and prepare a meal for Charles.

Sven had picked this up in his easy way and asked her who Charles was. "Oh, he's my son." She quickly made this mythical being into a fifteen-year-old, academic and thoroughly charming in manner and personality. He had accepted that she must go and cook for this paragon.

The next couple of days flew by as Meg went around in an apparent state of levitation. She prepared exceptional meals, so great was her confidence and joi-de-vivre she was bold enough to attempt recipes from the cordon bleu book Charles had given her last birthday. Charles was delighted and told her so. She found his praise very gratifying and accepted it as her due as she smiled at her husband.

Wednesday was bright and sunny, although intensely cold. Meg almost pushed Charles out of the house, scurried her way through the housework and then prepared the evening meal, leaving everything ready to switch on when she returned. She took a long, scented bath and lay in the soap bubbles planning her outfit. Gordon, she felt sure would be a very natty dresser and might well be sporting an embroidered waistcoat made by himself.

After much deliberation she was ready and set off for Sandford. Meg usually despised the houswifely chat shows on the radio, but this morning she felt so cheerful that she turned on the car radio and listened to the disc jockeys' inane chatter and laughed at his forced jokes.

It was just turned eleven as she drew up outside The Hare and Hounds. There was a man standing under the pub window, his dark hair blown about by the wind. He was trying to light a cigarette by using his jacket lapel as a wind shield. No embroidered waistcoat though. She took in the heavy knit pullover and tweed jacket. Very smart.

"Forgive me, but is it Lyz?" he was confidentiy opening the car door.

"How many women have you asked that of?" She laughed up at him.

"You're the first today." He helped her out of the car and waved away her apology for being late.

In no time she found herself behind a brandy and soda, divested of her coat and in the warm snug of the pub, without realising how she had been maneuvered into the position. My word, you're smooth, she thought, eyeing him over the top of her glass.

"I'm Gordon Hawkins," as he met her gaze.

"Lyz Goodricke, how do you do?" Meg felt his hand warm and firm in hers and experienced a quick thrill of excitement.

"Wednesday seems a rather unusual day off. Have you a business and work Saturday to have a mid-week day to yourself?"

"No, no business. I sometimes wish I had and then I would be my own boss. I work at the Infirmary in Wasterburn. We have a rota system and this week my day off is Wednesday."

"Embroidery is an unusual hobby for a man."

"Not really, I share it with several of my colleagues," he gave a deep chuckle, "I'm a surgeon." An excellent lunch was followed by a bracing walk round the botanical gardens.

Chapter 6

GORDON was very well informed about the heathers to be found in the rock gardens, he knew a great deal about an archaeological dig which a group of students was enthralled in uncovering in one corner of the botanical grounds. He seemed to never be at a loss for a word, never needed to say 'I don't know' or 'I'm not sure'. He was a veritable mine of information.

Towards the end of the afternoon, having been swept along by the charisma which surrounded Gordon, Meg took breath and began to wonder if she actually liked him as a person. She thought that she could find his assurance and his infallibility a trifle irritating. On the whole though, he proved to be a very entertaining character and they parted amicably with an agreement to meet the following week. Meg drove home in thoughtful mood, finding that the tide of good will which surrounded Gordon, quickly ebbed when he was gone.

Tomorrow was Thursday and the day she had agreed to meet the other Charles in Chester. Meg had no worries about confusing her appointments or forgetting anyone. She had the precise memory of the habitual liar. Apart from driving in the streets of Chester, which she intensely disliked, she was in two minds about this unknown Charles. He had seemed so unsure of himself, she had no desire to be cast in the role of agony aunt.

She and Charles had a quiet evening, the usual breakfast routine and Meg set off for another assignation with a strange man.

Meg immediately knew which was Charles. He stood, as nearly under the clock as was possible. Propped against the book stall he had a filleted look, as though unable to stand on his own. Oh Lord, she thought, this isn't going to be all beer and skittles. She was at once breezy, cheerful and organising.

"Are you Charles?"

"Yes, yes I am. Is it Lyz?" He struggled upright, the effort robbing him of further speech.

"Shall we go and have some coffee?" asked Meg. "This cold gets right into your bones." Charles livened up, said that the station coffee was awful but that he knew a reasonable cafe nearby. It was sure to snow soon, he added with an apprehensive look at the darkening sky.

The cafe was a five minute walk away during which she learnt that it was already snowing in Scotland, that it was forecast for Wales but might not reach across the Pennines until after the weekend. Meg also learnt that heavy floods had caused the cricket to be abandoned in Australia. The world weather situation had never been riveting as far as she was concerned, but Meg put up with it all philosophically, assuming that it was nervousness on his part, the casual chat of one stranger to another.

"You're a red-head," said Charles as she took off her coat and scarf in the over-warm cafe. Meg always liked to think of her hair as Titian rather than just plain red and felt rather cut up by his lack of finesse.

"You don't like red hair.?" It sounded cold and flat.

"I do, I do. It's a lovely colour. Like copper beech leaves." Meg looked at him from a new angle.

Charles explained, with much prompting and encouragement from Meg, that his business occupied much of his time. It was a grocery and off licence store. He opened early morning until late at night and took a few hours off in the middle of the day. This was to catch up on his housework, he explained. Meg felt she ought to apologise for taking him away from his ironing.

"Do you like being a shopkeeper? Don't you find the hours rather long?"

"It was my father's business," this by way of explanation. "Both my parents are dead." His sad, long face grew longer and sadder. "I've got a sister, she lives in Manchester. It always rains when I go to see her." He looked thoroughly miserable now. Meg felt if she drank any more coffee her hands would begin to shake.

"I've got a flat above the shop. Would you like to see it?" Meg recoiled thunderstruck at the sudden leer on Charles' face.

"Actually, I was thinking more in terms of a look around the Cathedral," she said coldly. From weather to Cathedral seemed more appropriate than weather to bed for first meeting. Charles withdrew again behind his solemn face.

His warning that the Cathedral would be cold proved to be correct. Stoutly denying feeling even chilly, Meg resolutely plodded round the church feigning interest in anything and everything. Charles trailed miserably behind, sniffing loudly and occasionally producing a sepulchral cough entirely in keeping with the gloom of the building. Hot tea and toasted teacake restored Meg's spirits somewhat. Charles was abject in his apologies. The proposed visit to his flat had only been a suggestion to get out of the cold, he assured Meg.

She accepted his explanation and, for some reason entirely beyond her understanding, agreed to meet Charles the following week. Their date was fixed for Wednesday. During the drive home she wondered what madness had possessed her that she should agree to meet this inadequate man again. She assumed it to be frustrated maternal inst incts. Nearing Castlebridge she brightened up remembering she was to meet Sven again.

Chapter 7

CHARLES had a slight cold on Friday morning, his car would not start and the cold tap to the bath was frozen up. Meg assumed that Charles would surrender to the fates and stay home for the day. She began planning how she could get away for a few hours in the middle of the day to meet Sven. Charles, methodical as ever, attached jump leads from her car to his and charged his battery. He took two aspirin for his cold; becoming more wretched by the minute; and told Meg she must ring the plumber and on no account tinker with the frozen pipe herself. Meg waved him off, no cheek brushing with a runny nose, and immediately plugged her hair dryer to 'warm' and held it under the pipe at the back of the bath. The obstruction cleared itself in a few moments. Meg did not think that hanging about waiting for a tradesmen to call was a day well spent. He would probably have seven reasons why he could not come and insist on telling her every one of them.

Sven was waiting at the Linden Tree, he looked fit and bronzed. Meg felt her heart leap into her mouth when she saw him. For his part he looked delighted to see her and laughed when she commented on his winter sunburn.

"It is the saunas, I go most evenings. They have a sun lamp I like to sit under. I wondered if you would like to go to the sauna this afternoon.

Meg had never counted modesty among her virtues and mixed bathing had always appealed to her. The vague appeal became what she must do immediately.

"I would love to go. Just what is involved?"

"First we go to the hot-house. There it is very warm and very much we sweat." It did not sound the most romantic way to spend an afternoon but she felt that sweating next to Sven could be heaven.

The sauna baths were situated in the grounds of an hotel on the edge of town. They took Sven's car and he sang to her in Swedish as they drove along. His voice was light but very pleasant. Meg asked for a translation of one song with a lovely melody but he said it was not a nice song and it would make her blush. This regard for her feelings seemed rather incongruous as they were on their way to a mixed bathing jaunt. The hot-house was very hot. Meg had thrown off her clothes with indecent haste and was lounging negligently against the extremely uncomfortable wooden boards near the hot stones when Sven came out of the changing rooms. She had been perspiring gently, as she looked at Sven's magnificent body she began to sweat profusely, every pore in her body opening like a flower in the sun.

He threw a bucket of water on the hot stones and, groping for her through the steam, he clutched her hand and sat down beside her.

"I hoped you would not be offended at my asking you to come here."

"Not at all, it's lovely." She dashed half a pint of moisture from her eyebrows.

"We go next to the cold showers."

"I'll look forward to that."

Meg wondered faintly if she would look ridiculous in her present naked state with her head between her knees. She gazed somberly at the widening puddle around her feet.

The cold baths were very cold. Meg stood on tiptoe to minimise the body area in contact with the icy swirls. Her breasts floated hugely on the surface and she hurriedly bobbed down in the water.

When she was wondering if she dare dive under the surface to search for her toes, which had become detached some time before, Sven waved at her from the other end of the pool.

He had swum up and down the pool several times as Meg stood, paralysed by the cold, her hands holding her nipple ends for fear they drop off. Sven had to shout twice down her ringing ears before she understood that they were to get out and go on to further joys.

"Outside we go now." Oh God, thought Meg. The freezing tour of the Cathedral with the drip-nosed Charles had been Valhalla to this. Clutching her hand Sven ran a marathon race across the gardens. The morning frost still kept the grass soldier -straight. Each blade like a bayonet beneath her bare soles. Meg detached herself from his grasp and let him stride off into the grey mist hanging dankly round the far hedges. The garden was completely enclosed and not visible from the road, a deliberate choice of location obviously.

Sven came bounding back, his damp hair curling round his ears. She was pretending an interest in a Christmas rose, struggling to bloom beside a holly bush.

"We go now and sun bathe." Meg looked desperately up to where the sun had been three months previously. "No, we go indoors again." Gratefully she followed. There were sun loungers around the walls of the room, the overhead heat was fierce. They lay, head to head along one wall and slowly cooked. The experience of the last hour was worthwhile for these moments of bliss. Sven was looking down at her with a faint smile on one corner of his mouth.

"You are ready?" Yes, I'm ready, she thought. Opening her eyes she saw that Sven was dressed. Meg scrabbled confusedly to her feet, stubbing her toe agonisingly on the table leg.

There was a licenced restaurant above the saunas. She buried her nose in the double brandy Sven set before her. It was pure nectar. Their eyes met as she looked up

"Your nose is red," laughing at her discomfort. "You have the skin to burn easily, the skin which goes with the red hair." Meg looked at him, she knew this of course and was always careful in the summer sun. He had told her that the saunas were not supposed to burn.

"My dog is a beautiful red-setter, his coat shines just like your hair." Remembering his devotion to his dog she decided that she must accept this as a compliment. Charles and the bathroom taps seemed miles away.

"My wife, she would not come here." Meg was back in this world again.

"How long have you been divorced now?"

"It is four years."

"What was the cause of the breakup?" It didn't seem impertinent to ask given the circumstances. He laughed and said it was a long story for another time.

"The children are the ones who suffer most. It was good that we had no children." His ex had obviously not fought for custody of the red-setter then. He was an easy talker, a good listener and time stood still while she was with him. She found that it had in fact flown. Meg told him of her wonderful son Charles and he accepted, as Gordon had done, that she must go home to this God-like being. Their parting was rather hurried but they made arrangements to meet again on the following Friday.

Chapter 8

THE Saturday sky was leaden and threatening. Charles did not look well. He sat at the breakfast table stabbing his fork at the scrambled egg, eventually breaking it into uncontrollable crumbs. Meg took it away without comment and poured more coffee. Charles drank like a legionnaire lost for days in the dunes. He decided against his usual walk and Meg offered to go to the library for him. Charles thanked her but showed no real interest in the books she brought for him. Mooning about the house he kept picking things up and putting them down again. Lunch held no interest. He sat trailing his spoon round the dish and making whorls in the custard. When treacle pudding did not appeal she knew that he was sick.

Charles took to his bed with very little protest. Meg made him comfortable with lots of drinks, tissues and fruit nearby. She put a book in his hand and advised him to go to sleep.

Meg went up with another cup of tea in the middle of the afternoon and found him sitting up and slurping noisily on an orange. His nose dripped rhythmically and the sodden tissue balls had grown until there was an arsenal like a snowball mountain on the bedside table. Meg shuddered, "I'b hab a sleeb."

She advised on the evening meal and Charles settled for soup. Setting a tray to take up to him, Meg sighed. She could see that it was going to be a very long weekend.

Charles accepted the turbid mixture she handed him for a night cap.

"Whad id id?"

"Aspirin." It was actually six aspirin mixed with two sleeping pills. Meg did not enjoy the role of sick nurse into which she was being cast. She certainly had no intention of being wakened in the night by Charles wanting anything.

Charles said he felt better in the morning but still rather 'waffy' and Meg thought he looked puffy round the eyes as though he had slept too deeply. She said further bed rest. Charles was hungry but she did not wait to see him clear his breakfast tray. He had an irritating way of scraping at the pattern on the bottom of the dish, as though there was nourishment to be had from the glazing. It was unbearable at the best of times.

Church did not really appeal but she went, really out of boredom and a desire to escape the house for a while.

Gilbert Crabtree, the vicar, was a born bachelor. It must have been obvious from the age of seven that he would never marry. His sister was his housekeeper, a dreamy creature who would appear at church functions, move, wraith-like among the parishioners and, just as suddenly, vanish without explanation. People often wondered if they had really seen her. Grace was forty-nine and had been so for the past twenty years. No-one called her by her first name, very few knew what it was.

Gilbert was also a very diffident man, shy at social encounters and keeping all casual acquaintances at arms length. Despite these short comings he was a warmly understanding man to parishioners in real need. It was as though he kept his reserves and cup of kindness replenished for these occasions. Meg was rather superior in her attitude toward him seeing him as a man doing a job and not doing it particularly well. Whether he kept God's house in good order was of no matter to her. Meg's reasons for going to church were certainly not religious. She called him Mr. Crabtree and was entirely patronising. Most people called him Gilbert, slapping him on the back and trying to draw him into social activities.

This morning he gave Meg a tight smile, hoped that Charles would soon be better. Meg thought he looked at her, from under his thick eyebrows in a calculating way, as if he knew all about her. Meg had once read that such eyebrows with ears that had no lobes, were characteristic of a criminal type. The vicar had no lobes to his ears. Reaching home Meg went straight upstairs to consult with Charles about lunch. She had to fight her way through a pall of pipe smoke hanging like a November mist around the bed. Charles' eyes were narrowed to peer between the lazy wreathes of smoke curling from his nostrils. Meg saw that the faint blue haze she had noticed on his chin the previous evening had become a navy gloss.

"If you get dressed Charles I'll tidy this room. He went grumbling off to the bathroom and Meg threw the window open.

Although an efficient and thorough housewife Meg always found the care of the sick distasteful. She invariably felt uncomfortable when she was near anyone who was ill.

She always ignored her own symptoms until they became a serious illness. Charles came out of the bathroom looking better and a light lunch was followed by an afternoon of playing scrabble and listening to music.

Meg was acutely bored but did not see what else she could do. Charles would not want her going off somewhere on her own and yet he would not agree to go out. Charles sniffed relentlessly. Meg felt trapped.

She cleared the meal away and went to take an early bath. Charles had left his towels from that morning on the floor in a sodden heap. She wearily picked them up and shuddered at the wash basin. He had shaken his razor into the bowl and the disgusting mess lay round the basin like black pepper.

The town was covered in a thick dazzling blanket of snow on the Monday morning and Charles decided to take the morning off. He ate a hasty breakfast and set to work to finish a marquetry picture he had started sometime during the summer holiday and worked on with loving care since then. The picture was of an unlikely looking fishing harbour. From his toneless whistling she assumed he was reasonably happy. Charles invariably finished off anything he started, it disturbed his sense of order to leave anything incomplete.

Meg was forever starting new hobbies but, once the initial phase of enthusiasm had abated, she lacked the stamina to complete them. The house was plentifully supplied with half finished pullovers, patchwork covers just begun, abandoned oil paintings sadly cracked. An incautiously opened drawer might tumble out a tapestry canvas or a chilly looking doll waiting to be dressed for the church fete. There had been an offer by Charles to frame any work she might finish. So far the only handwork on view was a five masted schooner assembled and painted by Charles. Meg admired the effort involved but would not say so for fear that he ought to help her finish a piece of work.

Chapter 9

ALTHOUGH Charles went to the office on Tuesday and Meg went to Barbara's for coffee and gossip with the girls she was very bored. The prospect of a meeting with Charles from Chester even began to look attractive. Tuesday evening brought torrential rain. Wednesday was bright, the evening rain having washed away the slush and given the town a newly laundered look. Charles' cold had left him with a troublesome cough but he armed himself with a proprietry cough balsam and set off for the office cheerfully enough. Meg did not give her husband a second thought once he was out of the house and set about getting ready to meet the other Charles in Chester. She had determined that, if he proved no more interesting than at their last meeting, then she would tell him there would be no more meetings.

Once again she found Charles propping up the book stall in his weary way. However, he seemed delighted to see her and was concerned and solicitous of her comfort; of her driving in such weather; that Meg warmed to him. Charles looked so serious and eager to please that Meg agreed to go with him and see his flat. It was only few minutes walk and it would be as well to leave her car in the park he said.

Meg was pleasantly surprised at Charles' shop premises, divided in two on a corner site. One half was a wine and spirits store.

"There's at least ten thousand pounds worth of booze in there," he said nodding to the heavily laden shelves. Meg could well believe it.

There was row upon row of expensive sherries, whisky and vodkas by the dozen and a whole row of Megs' favourite brandy.

"I wonder you don't get robbed," she commented as Charles led them into the other half of the shop.

"It's well protected," he laughed as he pushed the door. "These fellows won't let anyone in." Meg found herself looking into the eyes of two Doberman's. One dog raised his lip at her and made a faint rumbling in his throat.

"Quiet Rory, down." The dog crouched, head on his front legs and sneaked a glance at her from under his eyebrows.

"He won't really hurt you, he just looks fierce." The two dogs were now sat either side of Meg, curling their lips at her dangling fingers. She hurriedly crossed her arms

"People usually say 'he won't hurt you' just before their dog takes a steak-sized piece from a visitors leg." Laughing again Charles took hold of the dogs' collars and led them out to an enclosed yard at the back.

"There, I've shut them out. Shall we go upstairs and have something to drink, or would you like to see the shop first?"

Meg did not feel any interest in what she could now see was a general grocery store. She did though feel a reluctance to go immediately to Charles' flat.

"Do you keep all this on your own, you must be run off your feet?"

"I have a woman comes in to help on Saturdays, that's my busiest day, actually..." A sudden rush of confidence. "That was the reason I wrote to the bureau. I really need someone to help in the shop. Someone to work with me."

Meg wondered if a wife must be cheaper than employing a full time assistant. She picked up a tin of madras curry and put it down again, her eye catching a green glass jar filled with what looked like garden slugs.

"Snails, wholesale price to you." Realising he was serious about paying she chalked him up as mean, made no comment and moved round the other side of the counter.

"Careful. I was cleaning the bacon slicer and I haven't put the shield back on. It's very sharp," he added as Meg ran her thumb very gingerly along the blade. There were several kinds of cheeses, each under a little plastic dome of its' own. She saw her favourite Danish and wondered what he would charge for a tiny piece for her to take home.

"Mind there's a step, it's a bit dark at the back there, but if I put the lights on people will think I'm opening the shop and they'll come to the door. I don't open till half past three to catch all the mothers bringing kiddies from school. They always natter their mums for sweets." The previous suspicion that he was a scrooge was thus confirmed. She didn't think that he would make more than a few pence out of the infant lollies, but he obviously viewed each pint-sized customer as potential Rocker-fellers.

Finding the back of the shop too gloomy, Meg drifted behind the counter again. There was a sudden lull in the throbbing from the freezer and Meg turned to find herself staring at the knot in Charles' tie.

He was standing directiy in front of her, there was a faint aroma of cheese on his breath and it drifted toward her like a ghostly finger beckoning. Trying to back away, she found that the counter was pressing into her kidneys. Charles moved as she did, bringing his Camember breath even closer.

"I do like you Lyz," he reassured her. "I think you might be just the person I'm looking for to help me in the business." Meg felt she would be better able to appreciate the honour if the counter were not making her so uncomfortable.

"Charles, do let me out of this corner."

"Only if you pay a forfeit", he said playfully puckering his lips. Meg saw no way out but to kiss him, he wrapped his arms possessively round her as she did so. Great waves of cheesy bouquet poured down her neck as his breathing became more rapid.

"Come on Lyz, don't be stand offish. I know what red-heads are really like", he added with a nasty leer.

"Please let go Charles, you're hurting me. And rushing me," she hastened to add when she saw the determination in his face.

"Oh all right, but come upstairs. It's more comfortable up there." For what, she speculated. She realised that she was tantalising him when he made another lunge for her. His hands were very strong for such a weedy looking man.

"Do let loose, you're hurting." He slackened his grip on her upper arms. Meg wondered if bruises would show when she undressed that night.

Meg was irritated by his persistance and realised that there would be no let up unless she agreed to some compromise with him. If he could muster this much passion among the sides of ham and jars of snails, she knew he would not be deterred once they went upstairs.

"Aw, come on Lyz, be a sport." This silly expression annoyed her intensely, his breath repulsed her and the beads of sweat gathering on his eyebrows sickened her further.

"Let go," she spat at him fiercely. God, he was so stupid, he would not listen. Her irritation burst within her and she pushed him with all her strength. Charles fell back, he had been crouched over Meg, partly on his toes and she supposed he must have been off-balance to fall so easily. Meg watched the fall. He checked himself when he came to the step but was further tipped over by this obstruction and fell heavily across the counter. The blade of the bacon slicer bit deeply into his neck.

Chapter 10

THE bright arc of blood which rose from Charles' neck, terrified her. Her inherent horror of any kind of sickness rose to her throat and stemmed the already forming scream. Paralysed with fear she watched but not wanting to and yet unable to turn away. The fountain of blood continued to spurt, there was an obscene pulsing to it, which made it seem to dance to an unheard orchestral rhythm. Her face drained of colour; both hands pressed to her mouth to stem the rising tide of nausea; Meg watched. Her eyes stung with the effort of not blinking. Charles began to slip slowly, so slowly, to the floor. He fell heavily the last few inches and the thud roused Meg with a lurching jolt.

Noticing that her coat was stained with a thick, sticky substance Meg went toward Charles. Kneeling before him she put her face down and gazed into his surprised eyes, his face was ghastly pale. Feeling under his body, while trying to avoid the thin trickle still coming from his neck, she pulled one arm out. She felt for his pulse but could not find the faintest throb. Catching sight of the thick pool of dark blood on the shop floor, Meg felt no surprise at the realisation that Charles was dead. She pushed down on the rising panic within her, she felt as though she wanted to scurry into the furthest, darkest corner of the shop and there hide, pulling the darkness around her. An icy hand clutched her heart and spread its' fingers deep inside and up into her throat and with steady calm she took stock of the situation.

If she were to ring the police; she knew it was too late for a doctor; they would want to know about her involvement with Charles, her husband would be brought into the situation and Meg's world would crumble. They might suspect that she had deliberately set out to murder Charles, proving otherwise might be very difficult. Surely there would be no way of tracing her, it was unlikely that Charles had told anyone of his meetings with her.

Meg knew that there was nothing to be done for the man lying in a pool of congealing blood. It could not matter if the death was reported now, by her, or discovered later by someone else.

Picking up her bag and umbrella Meg made her way to the door, she had to fight to control her shaking fingers, but, at last, she had the catch of the door undone. A bell sounded like a death toll in her guilty ears and there was a low growling from a dog. Taking a deep breath Meg quickly pulled open the door and stepped out into the street. Without further hesitation and as rapidly as possible, she began walking to the shopping centre.

Reaching the end of the street she took off her coat and turning it the outside to the inside she draped it across her arm. How was she to get rid of it? How to explain the wet patches of blood, so obviously blood to her, but now drying to muddy brown.

The best way to hide a tree is in the forest. This silly phrase kept running through her head... the forest. To throw away a new expensive coat would be suspicious. A coat is not a tree, her mind spun off at tangents. Where would an article of clothing be unnoticed. In a clothes shop of course, but she could not take the coat back where it had been bought, certainly not in its' present state. Wash it? No it had a fur lining and would prove too difficult. A blinding flash of inspiration came to Meg. Of course, Hide a coat with other coats, she would take it to the dry cleaners. She was walking by the shops now and, as if in answer to prayer, she saw a Smiths cleaners on the other side of the road.

Weaving and dodging between the traffic, Meg made her way to the shop. She went in, holding her handkerchief to her face.

"I wonder if it's at all possible to clean this? I've had an awful nose bleed and made an awful mess." The assistant gazed dispassionately at the coat, holding it at arm's length.

"We'll try. I can't promise a good job. You might be better to have it dyed."

"I'll try the cleaning first and see how it comes up." Meg had no intention of ever returning for the coat, she only wanted rid of it. She gave the assistant an entirely fictious name and address. The girl handed her a ticket and smiled.

"You look very pale, not a bit well. It must have been a nasty nose bleed."

"I'm going home to lie down," was the response.

Feeling foolish and sure that everyone was staring at her, Meg walked through the streets with no coat and her umbrella raised against the drizzle. Reaching her car she sank gratefully into the driving seat, turning on the heater as she revved the engine. She was twenty odd miles out of the town before she was able to let out a deep and long held breath. With some surprise she saw that it was only three thirty. That so much could happen in so short a time astonished her, it seemed an age since she had set out for her meeting with Charles.

The house was very quiet and wrapped itself around her in welcome. Megs feet were leaden as she dragged them upstairs. 'Two vast and trunkless legs of stone stand in the something or other' she muttered turning on the bath taps and wishing she were back at school and learning poetry again.

Chapter 11

THE bath did little to ease the ache in her limbs and she realised it was the tense way in which she was holding herself, shoulders knotted, that was causing the aches. Dressed in casual easy clothes, she drifted round the house. Dust on the book shelves caught her eye and she hurriedly fetched cloths and polish. The shelves turned into the window sills and then the kitchen floor. It had been scrubbed that morning and certainly didn't need doing again. Sitting back on her heels she wiped her forehead with a grimy hand and felt sweat sticking her shirt to her back. She ran another bath. "I'm like Lady Macbeth," she thought as she scrubbed her hands. Charles arrived home after six. Meg ran to the door to meet him and flung her arms about him.

"Hey, steady, you'll have me on the floor." He gazed in astonishment at this departure from her usual routine. "You do look pale Meg, aren't you well?" He was kind, he was concerned and to Megs' astonishment she burst into tears.

"I expect you've been doing too much," as he led her to the settee. "I can smell the polish and everything looks lovely. You should get out more, Meg. Leave the housework.

Perhaps you've caught my cold, it made me feel rotten. Lie down and I'll get us something to eat." Meg renewed her sobbing.

"No," she howled, "There's a casserole in the oven. It's not much. I didn't feel..."

"Don't worry about it. I'll see to everything." His sympathy and warmth had unleashed the flood gates. The more he soothed the more the tears pumped out.

Meg had a misty vision of her father; who was very like Charles; sat astride a stool in their outhouse, a slaughtered pig across his knees, holding the head down so that the blood flowed from the neck to the bucket on the floor below. She turned back to her sobbing.

"Oh, Charles," she knew not whether she cried for the memory of the dead Charles or for the benefit of the living Charles. If he had been her father he would have patted her head and said 'there there, don't fret so'. Charles was made of sterner stuff. He helped her into bed, tucking her in all round as though she were in danger of falling out. Meg felt about six.

"I've had such a disappointment. I lost my coat. My new green one" she wailed. "I left it over my chair when I went to the lavatory in Malarkie's tea rooms. It was gone when I came back."

"Never mind, I'll get you another."

"You are good to me Charles."

"Not at all. Try and have a sleep now."

"I don't want another green one you know. Green coat I mean. I think green must be unlucky."

"You're probably right. Sleep now." Meg snuggled down, wriggling her bottom with the luxury and the safety of it all.

Meg woke the next morning to the sound of Charles gargling in the bathroom. It was a disgusting noise. He came breezily into the bedroom and enquired how she felt. Apart from a rather drained feeling she was well, the anxieties and tensions of the previous day had vanished with the morning sunshine. She immediately got up and began to prepare Charles' favourite omelette.

Charles was pleased that Meg was better and again promised to buy her another coat. Meg thought him sweet but was none the less eager to send him to the office. He finally went after Meg had promised to have an easy day and not overtire herself. He was barely up the garden path before she began her preparations to see Gordon. Gordon was waiting in the same place, he was wearing the same tweed jacket and was smoking. This time a very black looking cigar. There was an art exhibition at the local gallery and he suggested they go and see it.

"There are some good Turners being shown," he informed Meg.

"I love Art Galleries," she lied. The gallery was quite as boring as Meg had anticipated. Gordon, however, was his usual informative self. Meg decided that he was the kind of man who would know exactly where the candles and fuse wire were when there was a power cut. His infallibility was second only to that of the Pope.

Gordon chose to eat at an Italian restaurant on the other side of town and they set off at a cracking pace through the shopping centre.

Meg was beginning to wonder if they would have curried donkey on the menu, she was so hungry when they arrived she was sure she could eat one. Slightly out of breath she told Gordon that she would have whatever he was ordering. He doubled his order without asking if she liked his choice or not.

It was an extremely well-cooked meal, the waiters were attentive without being obsequious. The bottle of wine they shared was not too heavy, not too warm. Everything was so perfect that Meg began to wonder again about the smooth, sure way which hung like a cloak about Gordon's shoulders. Nothing disturbed him, everything moved on oiled wheels wherever he turned. Meg speculated why such a God-like being should feel the need to write to a marriage bureau. Surely every woman at the hospital must fall at his feet in admiration when he walked their way. Throughout the day Meg had resolutely ignored the events of the previous day. She would not allow them to rise to the surface of her conscious mind. Always a firm believer in the maxim that to ignore something was to make it disappear, she was able to obliterate memories of Charles lying dead on the floor with little difficulty. Her conscience was clear, there was no reason to be involved in the death of a shop-keeper who was virtually unknown to her. It was nothing to her, she reasoned. Until she bought a newspaper on the way home.

Gordon had been very charming, very talkative and told Meg about his mother, the only family he had left. The old lady lived on Wales and he saw her infrequently although she wrote long rambling letters telling him to wear warm underwear and not smoke cigarettes. He reassured her that he did all she advised. He didn't seem to need any contribution to the conversation from Meg. It was mostly a monologue of his virtues. The delight of his mothers' eye, pride of his school and the best surgeon who ever threaded cat-gut at the infirmary. Why then should such a paragon need to write to a marriage bureau? She decided to leave this question for another time and arranged to meet the following week. She was very thoughtful on the way home. Stopping for petrol at the garage on the outskirts of Castlebridge Meg saw that the early evening papers were on the news stand. Putting her fifty pence piece in the cup on the stand she picked up a paper and began to read of Charles' death. She had read two paragraphs before she related the article to the events of the previous day. There was an unreality about it that Meg found her traumatic experience unable to correlate with the reporters' account of the happenings. The body of Charles Rogerson, she read, had been discovered by Mr. Sam Leibits, a commercial traveller for a firm of whisky manufacturers. Mr. Leibits had become concerned for the safety of Mr. Rogerson when there had been no answer to the doorbell. He had thought it strange that the shop was closed at ten in the morning and the dogs had been barking in the back yard. Hungry, thought Meg.

The newspaper went on to describe how the body was lying in a pool of congealed blood, that the dogs were locked in the yard and were howling 'like the banshees' said the paper. From the condition of the body it was thought that he had been dead some time. A post-mortem examination would establish the exact time and cause of death.

Meg felt sick, she had not realised there would be such a full investigation. In her cloud-cuckoo land she had somehow assumed that, once the police realised it had been an accident, they would want the funeral arrangements to go ahead as soon as possible. Yet here they were, messing about with a dead body as though it were a possible murder. The police are pursuing their enquiries, she read a cold hand clutching her heart.

"The police came to see me today." The cold hand clutched tighter. "I had a slight accident. I didn't tell you yesterday as you were so upset. There was no real damage done but I knocked down a bollard as I turned the corner by the British Legion Club. I had a narrow escape really." You and me both, thought Meg.

"It's a nasty corner, all the winds of the world seem to blow on it and it's slippery when the rest of the ice has melted away," she commented.

"The car wheels just spun round. Anyway the police say I have to pay for the bollard. No damage to the car of course." With a bumper such as he had on his Volvo it was not a surprise.

"I brought a late paper in with me. The headlines are all about some butcher who fell in the mincer and killed himself."

"Grocer."

"Sorry?"

"Grocer, he was a grocer and he fell onto the bacon slicer."

"Gruesome anyway. How do you know so much about it?"

"I bought a paper earlier and it caught my eye."

"Caught his neck apparently and it severed his jugular vein. Blood on the ceiling according to the man who found him." Meg protested faintly.

"Sorry, dear. I forgot you weren't feeling well. Must say you look better today. Bit of a smokey smell about you. You haven't started smoking?" He laughed.

"No, of course not. Barbara has gone back to it though. She's started smoking some weird French brand. Not very pleasant." She hoped this would explain the cigar smell from Gordon.

"Peter won't like that. He lectures on the evils of cigarettes." Meg busied herself with the meal and tried to dismiss all intrusive thoughts about dead grocers and police investigations.

When Meg set off for Sandford on the Friday morning it was as though a whole life time of events had been packed into the previous week since her last meeting with Sven. The sight of his open, honest face cheered her enormously. His first words deflated her instantly.

"I have to go to an inquest next Friday, perhaps I could see you some evening instead."

"Oh, no," she gasped.

"Why not? I would not keep you out too late, you could get back to your son at a reasonable time, I expect he worries."

"I meant 'oh no' about the inquest. Has someone died who you knew well, a relative?"

"Not at all. He was only an acquaintance. A customer of mine in Chester."

"Chester?" hoarsely.

"Yes, he was found dead in his shop, and as I was there that morning, the police want me to be at the inquest to say how he seemed to be recently. They want I think, for me to be able to say that he was cheerful and then it will be an accidental death. They do not want it to be suicide."

"Suicide?"

"It's not really very likely. He died after cutting his neck on a bacon slicer. I think there must be easier ways to end your life."

"I didn't know your round went as far as Chester."

"Ye, I have a two hundred mile radius. Chester is well within my boundary. It was sheer chance I called on Chuck Rogerson that day though."

"He was a grocer wasn't he? I thought you were a drug rep."

"That's right, but I also have medical supplies." He grinned broadly. "Lyz wake up I also supply contraceptives to all kinds of shops and businesses. This is not good we can talk about something more cheerful than Chuck Rogerson dying."

"Chuck?"

"That was his name. It's short for Charles I understand. Of course! Your son is Charles, do you ever call him Chuck?"

"Absolutely not," with some asperity.

"There's an Art exhibition. Would you like to go and see it?"

"I think not," with a decisive snap.

"You don't like paintings?"

Not twice in two ruddy days I don't, she thought.

"Actually, I've seen it." Charles brought me, she explained. "There are some good Turners," she added knowledgeably. Meg did not know a Turner from a Picasso.

Chapter 12

SVEN finally took her to the archaeological 'dig' in the botanic gardens. This was the one on which Gordon had commented so cleverly but she didn't think she could give a thumbs down sign to everything Sven suggested. She suffered the trip philosophically and was able to remember some of the comments Gordon had made. Sven looked at her in admiration and she became quite eloquent on the subject of early Scandinavian settlements.

Meg could feel the animal magnetism of the man and yet he seemed completely impervious to her. He had taken her hand on a couple of occasions but it was out of polite consideration. A hand given in friendship to help over rough places where she might stumble. She felt increasingly frustrated, she desperately wanted him to notice her. She knew that, were he to ask or to demonstrate the need ,then she would become his lover.

Sven laughed at her cold hands and reddened face and, taking pity on her, took her back to the Linden Tree for tea. Meg chased the buttered muffins with scalding tea and smiled gratefully at Sven over her cup.

"You are like a little girl, sitting like that." Meg had her legs hooked around the underneath rungs of the chair to keep them out of the way of possible draughts.

"There is butter on your chin." Meg immediately felt gauche, put her feet on the floor and wiped her chin.

"Why did you never marry again when your husband died?"

The topic of her supposed widowhood had never arisen before and Meg tried desperately to think of something plausible that could have brought Charles' life to such an untimely end.

"When Charles died I had been nursing him for so long and I was just so exhausted that the matter never entered my head until recently, five years after his death," she added.

"He was ill for months and the strain was dreadful, Brain tumour," she elaborated, her eyes becoming dark and brooding with the painful memories. Sven took her hand and she squeezed a tear to prolong the contact a little longer.

"I'm sure you were a devoted nurse."

"I did my best for him." The poignancy of the freshly minted memories stirred her anew and she bit her lip to avoid an embarrassing show of emotion. A mental image of herself wearing a starched and fluted cap flashed before her. The image was too hazy to see whether the tranquilly folded hands held a lamp or not. The reality that she was unable to clean up after herself when she was sick was a fact she firmly suppressed.

"Little Charles was only ten when his father died, it isn't easy bringing up a boy on your own," her swimming eyes would have melted the heart of an inquisitor.

"More tea?" He was obviously one of the mountain of people who think that grief can be dulled by food. Meg shook her head, withdrew her hand and stood up.

"I must go."

"But we haven't arranged our meeting yet. Could it be an evening next week?"

"Oh, well I don't know...Yes all right." She was suddenly decisive. Charles would have to put up with it. "Yes, Sven, I will meet you next week. Which evening would be best?"

"I'm in your hands." Oh I wish you were, she thought. They agreed on Wednesday at eight.

"The sauna again," suggested Meg. "I did enjoy that." Surely it could not have been as exhausting as she remembered it? Sven laughed delightedly and squeezed her hand. His eyes looked down into hers and , for one breathless moment, Meg thought that he was going to kiss her. She half closed her eyes in expectation and prepared to melt in his arms. Sven tweaked her nose, took her hand and led her to the door. Hot tears of disappointment came to her eyes as she stumbled after him from the cafe.

Sven handed her carefully into her car, stepped back and waved cheerfully at her. Meg swallowed hard, showed him all her teeth in a brief dazzle and shot off without a backward glance.

As she savagely ground her way through the gears Meg bit back her tears of frustration and resolved that she must find what it was she wanted from their relationship. Or what it was that Gordon wanted for that matter, she thought.

As she turned into the gates of the house she saw with horror that Charles' car was parked on the drive, not very well parked she noticed absently. She re-arranged her face, instantly remembering that Charles had encouraged her to go out more and, after all, he could not possibly know where she had been. Or could he? She cheerfully shouted his name as she let herself into the house. There was no answer. Puzzled at the silence, she made her way upstairs, calling as she glanced in the spare room where Charles kept his hobby equipment and peered in the bathroom. The answering quiet she found rather disturbing.

Chapter 13

CHARLES was lying on top of the bed, the travelling rug, which Meg kept on top of the blanket chest, was across his knees. His eyes were half closed and his breath came in great rasping gasps, at each indrawn breath his hands convulsively grasped the rug.

"Charles, whatever is it?" she went down on one knee and peered up into his face, which was almost slumped onto his chest.

"Not well. Came home early, couldn't bear it. Feel terrible." He sounded like a text message, each word delivered independently of the next.

"I'm going to ring Doctor Bickerdyke, just lie still and I'll be back directly." Charles nodded, he didn't look as though he wanted to get up and defy Meg. The doctors' number was engaged, patiently Meg broke the connection and dialed again. At the third try she got through and as calmly as possible described Charles' symptoms to the receptionist.

"Someone will be with you as soon as possible," said the tight voice at the other end. Meg rang off without further comment. She propped the front door open, turned on the hall light for the doctor, the winter evening was very gloomy. Meg went back to Charles whose eyes seemed to be sunk into his skull and his cheek bones shone a grey-white colour

"Doctor will soon be here," she tried to sound reassuring and Charles smiled wanly at her. The grin was immediately wiped off his face as he tried to take another croaking lungful of air.

Meg went into the bathroom to find a face cloth. She had a vague idea that she should mop Charles' brow. Perhaps that was when you had been shot by the Indians and the arrow was still lodged in the chest wall?

The doctor was running two at a time up the stairs as she came out of the bathroom. Meg pointed at the bedroom door.

"Now then, old chap, much pain?"

"Pretty bad doctor."

"Let's have a look at you." He rubbed his stethoscope on his own knee and then planted it firmly on Charles' chest with the directive that Charles take deep breaths. Meg hovered uncertainly round the bed but collected herself together enough to help sit Charles up in bed while the doctor listened to his back.

"Hmm, you've had a nasty cold and neglected it. It's taken a firm hold and settled a lot of rubbish at the bottom of your lungs. I'll give you an injection now and a prescription for some antibiotics. Could you see to getting it made up?" he asked Meg.

"Of course doctor," she smiled bravely at him.

"There's a chemist on Market Street, do you know it?"

"Oh yes." She led the man downstairs. He picked up his overcoat and looked steadily at Meg.

"Your husband has pneumonia, probably caused by neglecting a cold," his tone was accusatory. "However, it will clear up with the medicine. A better diagnosis than the one I was thinking when I got your message. I was sure from the symptoms you described that he was having a coronary."

Doctor Bickerdyke sounded as though it was Meg's fault that Charles was not as sick as the doctor had hoped. Words of apology came to her lips. She bit them back.

"I'll pop in tomorrow but meanwhile keep him warm, light diet and see that he has his pills as prescribed."

"Thank you for coming. I'm very grateful." This polite pleasantry fell from her lips with no effort. Her mind was racing ahead on other topics. Was it possible that he could have a coronary? Meg knew little about such things but she had read articles in the popular magazines. Reviewing the knowledge that she had, she realised that Charles was indeed the type; if type there were; to fall victim. His age was right, his sedentary job, he was a worrier and about a stone overweight. Meg was very thoughtful as she went upstairs. She helped Charles into bed properly, turned the heat up a few degrees and told him she would be as quick as possible getting his medication. Charles closed his eyes and nodded wearily.

The pharmacy was crowded and she was told the dispenser would be about twenty minutes before he got around to making up the prescription. She said she would be back and decided, on impulse, to go to the library.

The library was also crowded. Did no-one go to the theatre or to shows any more? She quickly found the medical books. 'You and Your Coronary' looked promising and another fat tome with the irrefutable title 'Heart Disease Kills' were just what Meg was looking for. She picked up a hobby book and a cowboy for Charles, checked them all out and returned to the pharmacy.

The instructions were printed neatly on the bottle and Meg dutifully roused Charles at eight o'clock. He swallowed two of the capsules Meg gave him, drank a pint of juice and promptly went back to sleep again.

Meg made herself a sandwich, toyed with and rejected the idea of a brandy to wash it down. She knew her alcohol consumption was increasing, vowed to curb her drinking and made a pot of tea.

She fetched the library books and propped the thickest tome against the tea-pot.

Chapter 14

MUCH of the book made very dry reading, but Meg had the ability to sift the facts, retain the essentials and to reject what was, to her, inconsequential nonsense. She became increasingly thoughtful as she read, realising the extreme frailty of the human body and the number of ills to which it might fall prey.

The symptoms she had described when she rang the surgery were indeed those of a heart attack. She learnt that a coronary was often diagnosed on the symptoms alone. It was not until the patient was hospitalised that a more accurate diagnosis could be made with the help of the cardiograph machine. If the patient did not make it to the hospital then the diagnosis was made on symptoms alone and the doctor had no hesitation in writing a death certificate.

Doctors, she read, only refused to give a certificate if they were unsure of the cause of death, or if they had not been in attendance on the patient in the recent past. Meg was very thoughtful as she turned the pages. If, she concluded, the doctor were visiting a patient and the patient were to die then the doctor would almost certtainly write a certificate perhaps even out of pride, a reluctance to admit that he didn't know what was the cause of death. A doctor would only accept the signs given by the patient but would probably take the word of a close relative.

Rousing Charles at midnight, Meg offered him his medication. Charles was cross at being wakened and angrily pushed Meg's hand away as she held out the capsule. Sod you, she thought, I couldn't care less if you take them.

Lying wide awake by Charles' side, Meg looked over the events of the day. She had experienced that now familiar thrill of spending a few hours with Sven and then coming home to the reality of Charles' illness. If it really had been a heart attack instead of a boring chest infection, then she might have been free to pursue Sven. As sleep crept in little whirls around her feet and up through her body Meg began to acknowledge the thought that she was disappointed at Charles not being whisked off with a massive coronary. Meg knew that Charles carried a heavy insurance policy; after all he would know better than anyone which was good value. If Charles were to die then Meg would be quite a comfortably well-off widow.

The nibbling thoughts had now caused an erosion and Meg drifted into sleep with a mental image of herself dressed in black- it had always looked startling with her colouring- a delicate handkerchief held to her face. Watching a lot of late night films on the television had brought home to Meg that widows always looked very attractive. The doctor arrived very early, before morning surgery thought Meg. She wondered if this was a yard stick by which you might judge how sick a patient was. A visit before nine must surely mean that the doctor was a little anxious about Charles.

"He had a very restless night and still complains of chest pain." Meg looked the doctor straight in the eye.

"Hmm," non committally.

"I've been sponging him down, he was sweating such a lot during the night." She thought that was enough symptoms from 'You and Your Coronary'

"Yes, there's very little you can do really. He is managing the antibiotics all right and plenty of fluids?"

"Oh, yes doctor, he's taking them every four hours," she lied in her most horror-stricken voice. Surely he didn't think Charles was lacking in attention her spaniel look plainly said.

Doctor Bickerdyke came downstairs biting his lip, he squared his shoulders and took a deep breath. "I'm wondering if your husband might be better in the hospital. There should have been some response to the antibiotics by now, he's had what, three lots?"

"Four doctor, eight last night, midnight, four in the morning and again at eight this morning." She would never have roused herself at four in the morning to see to him even if she loved Charles dearly, which she didn't.

The doctor seemed to accept that his word was law and that Meg had been following his instructions to the letter.

"This is putting a tremendous strain on his heart, Mrs. Goodrick, but I'll leave it for now if you think you can cope?"

"Oh yes doctor, it's no trouble to me, I just want to see Charles getting better. He seems to be in such pain," her lower lip trembled. The doctor was still young enough to be embarrassed by women on the verge of emotional outbursts.

"Must get on," he grunted. "Will call back this evening." The doctor's car roared off and Meg hugged herself. The silly fool must think that Charles is in real danger, he would hardly call twice in one day if he were satisfied with Charles' condition.

Finding Charles asleep again Meg sat in the bedroom armchair and gazed at her husband. There had never been a time when Charles looked attractive when asleep, his lower jaw jutted forward and his mouth dropped open in natural sleep. Now he had added an unattractive drool and a wheezy snort when he breathed in. His navy blue chin and tousled hair further repulsed Meg.

As though sensing that he was being watched Charles opened one eye, the other was bunged up with sticky gunge which Meg felt quite unable to wipe away.

"Need go lavatory" he said in his text speak.

"Lie still, I'll get you the bottle." Meg had found the urinal last night in the spare bedroom, she remembered they still had it, a relic from the brief spell Charles' father had stayed with them before being taken into hospital where he had died after some dreadful bowel operation. The old man had used the bottle during the nights and left it on the bedside table for her to empty in the mornings. Meg had found it a repulsive task, had told Charles so and he had taken over the job. The bottle, an air ring, and a bed cradle had all been left when the old man died, forgotten relics of a solitary visit by a red-cross nurse.

Chapter 15

MEG saw to Charles' needs with mechanical rapidity and no tenderness. She even -gritted her teeth and wiped his sticky eye. His pyjama jacket was stiff with the accumulated dried dribble of the night before and this she changed for him. She thought all the effort would impress the doctor. The clean jacket was a pale green and gave him a ghostly glow as the light reflected the colour onto his face. It was an unhappy choice but she didn't feel she could be bothered to change it again. Charles wouldn't want her to, it had exhausted him, besides it would be best that the doctor saw him as ill looking as possible. Nothing would then be a surprise to him. Nothing at all. Charles drowsed his way through the day, his breathing seemed to be more laboured as the day went on. The sewing lay on Meg's lap and the gloom of the winter evening crept across the bedroom floor. It was only three o'clock when she turned the light on.

She stood the lamp on the floor near her chair so that the reflected light did not disturb Charles. Meg had no real concern for the sick man but thought it would look more considerate on her part when the doctor returned. She thoughtfully turned on the hall and landing light for the doctor and settled back in her armchair. A tentative plan was forming in her head, it had no definite shape as yet. Wait for the doctor and play it by ear was the policy she decided on.

True to his word the doctor arrived, breezy as ever. He began gnawing his lip again as he entered the bedroom and heard Charles breathing.

"Been like this long?"

"Just about an hour since the last lot of capsules at four o'clock, he vomited them back again," she fantasised, remembering another symptom from her current favourite book.

There was no response from the doctor, he leant over Charles, stethoscope roaming over his patients' chest. Meg followed him to the bathroom where he scrubbed his hands as though he were about to remove Charles' appendix for want of something more concrete to do.

"I'm not too happy about the way things are going," he said, shaking soap suds over Meg as she passed him a towel. "Not at all happy," he added by way of emphasis.

"What is the trouble doctor?" gazing with troubled eyes into the pale orbs of the young man.

"The lack of response to the antibiotics is putting extra strain on his heart. I think there is some indication of right ventricular failure," he was obviously thinking aloud trying to formulate his thoughts.

"Ventricular?"

"Sorry I didn't mean to worry you, it is rather complicated, you wouldn't understand."

"No doctor," said Meg dutifully. The words ventricular failure had seemed like the fluttering of angel's wings.

Really Charles was becoming rather tiresome, why did he have to drag things out so.

"I can't understand why he hasn't responded to the drugs." You wouldn't respond if you hadn't been given them you fool. She smiled wanly and agreed that it was very worrying.

"If there's no change by tomorrow morning I'll get him into the hospital. I'm sorry my dear," seeing Megs lip quivering. "It really will be for the best. I can get him on a defibrillator there," he added to himself. Not if I can prevent it said Meg to herself.

"Goodbye and thank you." The little catch in her voice added, she thought, just the right touch of concern and bravery.

With the doctor gone, Charles fell asleep and, in the winter evening quiet Meg began her preparations.

Firstly, it was necessary to check with the medical books once more. She wanted all symptoms and the course of the disease firmly etched in her mind. Coronary arteriosclerosis, she read. Primarily a disease of middle age, but becoming more prevalent in younger age groups. Exacerbated by stress, overweight and strain such as smoking or chronic or untreated chest infections. Symptoms were often sudden in onset, acute in nature and often culminated in sudden death. Recovery was possible if treatment was instituted early enough, although the danger of further attacks was possible.

Meg knew that the pneumonia could not be guaranteed to kill Charles, even when left untreated. He would definitely have to be given a helping hand.

Collecting all the left-over sleeping capsules, which were tucked away in drawers and cabinets about the house, Meg began her preparations. She painstakingly opened all the capsules onto a piece of writing paper. Some capsules were blue, some green and there were several large red ones. The collected powder made a satisfying mound on the paper. The coloured gelatine containers she flushed down the pan. Removing the bottle of antibiotics from Charles' bedside Meg also emptied the contents of these capsules down the lavatory, saving the red and black gelatine containers Meg then began the tricky task of filling the antibiotic capsules with the sleeping powders.

With patient packing and constant tamping down of the contents with the knob end of a knitting needle Meg found that she was able to pack about the powder from six sleeping pills into two antibiotic capsules. It was a laborious task and took a long time. Eventually there were six antibiotic containers into which she had packed, possibly twenty sleeping powders.

Chapter 16

IT was nine o'clock when Charles woke and asked for a drink and the urinal.

"It's eight o'clock," she told him. "You must try and take your medicine." Charles nodded in agreement. "Three?" he queried as Meg dropped the capsules into his hand.

"Doctor increased them, you've got a nasty bout of flu," the answer was pat and reassuring.

"Rotten," he agreed and closed his eyes as Meg took away the jug of fruit juice. At ten o'clock, a brief hour later, Meg roused Charles again, this time with some difficulty.

"I'm sorry to have to wake you darling, but you must have your next dose of medicine."

"Time s'it ?" he slurred.

"It's midnight, I'm sorry but I'll have to wake you again at four, doctor was most insistent about every four hours." Charles nodded, too tired to protest. He was asleep again almost before he had swallowed three more capsules. Gazing down on her ashen grey husband Meg began to worry. Her worries were not those of a stricken conscience, nor were they anxieties about any suffering she might be causing Charles. Her only concern was whether or not the sedatives she had given Charles would be a fatal dose.

Thumbing through the text book she found 'barbiturate overdose'. Methods to aid recovery were described but there was no mention of what constituted a lethal dose.

A sudden panic gripped Meg. What if Charles were to recover? What if he were to be taken unconscious to hospital? Doctor Bickerdyke, fool though he was, would be sure to question the reason for his patient being comatose. What if Charles were to get better to tell the tale of taking so much medicine. No, that would not matter, he was really too disorientated to realise how Meg was telescoping the time lag for him. He had accepted that Meg was looking after him and presumably giving him the meds as prescribed. Charles' state of mind did not matter too much, what would be worse would be her sheer frustration at seeing him recover. If Charles were to be seen by the doctor in his present state the doctor would be sure to insist on a whole barrage of tests and investigations. She must make absolutely sure that Charles was quite dead when seen by the doctor. Oh, if only she could be certain that the barbiturates were enough, or rather, too many.

With a flash of unaccustomed affection Meg remembered her father-in-law. He had been a co-operative old man toward the end, had lapsed into unconsciousness and died immediately after his operation. Neat and tidy on the whole, no prolonged illness and exhausting weeks of waiting for the end. There had been a time, before his hospital admission, when Charles and the doctor had been trying to persuade him to have the operation. Now he had been a nice doctor, the senior partner in the practice where Doctor Bickerdyke now was. He only attended a select few of his patients, ones with whom he had a long association.

Charles' father had been one of these and Doctor Rees had been kindness itself to the old man. They had been two comrades united against common enemies, age, pain and death. Not that he had been allowed to have any pain, Doctor Rees had seen to that. A mental image flashed before Meg of Charles tucking a box away on top of the wardrobe in the spare room his father had occupied. It was out of reach of the old man and yet there if needed.

Meg remembered the doctor explaining to Charles about it. Pethidine had he called it? Not being interested in the details of sickness Meg had not listened to the conversation. Charles told her later that his father could have an injection if he felt any pain. She had promised Charles that she would ring Nurse Danby or go across the road for Miss Parsons, who was a retired nurse and would give the injection if necessary. The little box had never been opened. Meg knew this because she had discovered the box during her Spring cleaning. Charles had taken it from her and commented that he ought to return it to the surgery. It had never been mentioned again but she felt sure it had not been returned.

Now that must have been a powerful drug because Charles had told her at the time that his father was not to have more that one injection in four hours. She realised that she had been praying for access to dangerous drugs a few minutes before. If she could just find that box perhaps inspiration would come to her.

Charles was something of a squirrel and kept all manner of, to her, useless objects. His hobby-cum-spare room was the most likely place for anything valuable and she knew that he would class the little box as valuable. Really his lock-up drawer or the back of his wardrobe would be the most likely place.

Charles did not stir when she went into the bedroom for his key ring. It was lying on the dresser among the loose change from his pockets, his pipe was spilling tobacco onto the polished surface. Picking up the keys, she glanced at Charles. His breath came in long, deep snorts and sounded wet and thick at the back of his throat. Meg gazed at him with distaste.

Ignoring the car keys, Meg grasped the little brass key next to the front door key and put it in the bureau drawer. It opened easily and suddenly, spilling a paper bag onto the floor. Picking it up she glanced curiously inside. There was a locket on a thin gold chain. There was another bag, this one marked with the name of a well-known jeweller and containing a brooch with delicate silver work on the face. Meg flushed as she remembered. Charles had taken her to town to choose a watch for her birthday, last year or the year before. They had gone home and, in a rush of confidence, Meg had shown Charles the locket, explaining that she had 'borrowed' it from the shop. Charles had been horrified and not at all impressed with her sleight of hand. He said that, had she told him she wanted the locket, he would have bought it for her. There was no need to STEAL it he had said in capital letters. She had answered casually that she didn't want it now but had wanted to see if she could get it out of the shop.

Chapter 17

MEG had immediately forgotten the trinket and had never thought what had happened to it. In a vague way she had assumed that Charles had made it right, had settled it all with his annoying conscience. She had once seen him put two ten-pound notes in the collection plate in church. When she had asked why he had shushed her and whispered 'conscience money' and carried on singing the hymn as though he had not a care in the world.

The brooch was one she had bought for herself and almost immediately lost it. He must have confiscated it thinking she had lifted it. It had been rather expensive and she had bought it with her winnings from a horse called Church Mouse which had romped home at very long odds. She had not told Charles about backing horses, she knew he would not approve. There was so much of which he disapproved. The little brown box was at the back of the drawer. Presumably Charles had put it there for safety and forgotten about it. Doctor Rees. Thornhill House was written on the lid. This was scribbled out and Charles Goodricke Senior written in red pen. Meg found two hypodermic syringes in plastic envelopes, three needles each in its own plastic bubble. Carefully lifting out the cotton packing, she found three glass phials, each containing a bubble of turbid liquid. Pethedine 50mgs, she read on the side of each one.

Of nursing Meg had no knowledge, of the practicalities of nursing and injection techniques she knew more, only due to having watched Doctor Bickerdyke as he had given Charles the antibiotic injection. She had already decided that she would give Charles the pethedine. Presumably it was no good giving it by mouth, it must be more effective by injection. Her brief knowledge, gleaned from watching the doctor, would have to do. This must in fact be easier because she had seen him introduce some water into the phial and mix it with the antibiotic powder. This stuff was obviously easier as it was already mixed.

Emboldened by her success with the sleeping powders and her determination giving her courage, Meg took the box and its' deadly contents upstairs. Charles lay slumped over the bed one arm trailing down the side. He was breathing more quietly now, his nostrils dilating with every breath, his nose very prominent. There was a bubble of saliva at the corner of his mouth.

"Charles," her voice was sharp and sounded very loud to Meg in the still room.

"Charles," louder this time. There was no response. She hissed in his ear and the bubble of saliva burst at the corner of his mouth.

Satisfied that he would not open his eyes to watch her, Meg began her preparations. She took and tapped each of the pethedine phials until the contents gelled together at the bottom of the glass and then, with some difficulty, she snapped the narrow end of each little bottle.

Failing to separate the plastic around the syringes, she tore at them with her teeth, the needles had pull-off ends revealing a coloured surround designed to fit the end of the syringe. So far so good. Drawing the medicine from the phial and up the barrel of the syringe was not as easy as it had seemed when she watched the doctor. At last it was done and the contents of the three miniature bottles were drawn up into one syringe. Carefully holding it, that not a drop be lost, she approached the bed. With an inner lurch of guilt and apprehension, she found herself gazing into Charles' wide open eyes. She smiled tremulously at him. Charles focused on some point beyond her left shoulder.

"It's four o'clock," she said inconsequentially. Charles gazed unwinkingly at the curtain pelmet. "Time for more medicine," she added. Charles expressed no opinion on the matter. On the pretext of holding his hand Meg felt for a pulse. There was no answering throb under her fingers. Meg was not sure this was a good guide anyway as she could not often find her own pulse.

Holding her cheek near Charles' mouth she felt his breath faintly on her face. Finding his unwinking stare rather disconcerting, she tried to turn him over. She was seeking the tiny puncture hole in his right buttock where he had been given the previous jab by the doctor. Meg had some idea of trying to use the same site and thus cover her own tracks should there be an examination after. After what? Well AFTER.

Trying to turn Charles proved to be impossible. Crossing his legs and twisting his shoulders just seemed to put him in an ungainly knot. She wrapped her arms about him and tried to move him by brute force. This made the blood in her head sing and she fell across Charles gasping and giggling. He continued his abstract examination of the curtain track. She thought she detected an expression of surprise in the curl of his lip.

"Charles, do help dear," she gasped. "I'm trying to turn you over." The man on the bed looked more than ever like Oliver Hardy and more than ever determined not to help his wife in her devious plans.

"Charles, you pudding," she snapped. How bitterly she regretted all those treacle sponges she had encouraged him to eat.

After twenty minutes Charles still lay obstinately on his back and Meg sat on the carpet panting and hating her husband wholeheartedly because he would not help her to kill him.

Chapter 18

THE ludicrous situation again struck Meg as being comical and she burst into a further attack of giggling. Charles did not laugh. When she looked again his eyes were closed. With a feeling that it might be a prelude to recovery, she became instantly resolute.

Grasping the syringe firmly Meg rolled back the bedclothes, pulled at Charles pyjama trousers, wriggled them until she had a view of his bottom. With only a brief hesitation she plunged the needle home. He did not jump and made no effort to pull away. She held him firmly and pushed the plunger of the needle as far as it would go. A tiny bead of blood appeared as she took out the syringe. Doctor Bickerdyke had a tiny medicated swab with which he had wiped the site, Meg made do with a Kleenex tissue and, as she pressed on the spot, the bleeding stopped. Kneeling on the carpet, she closely examined Charles' bottom. There was really nothing to see and Meg felt proud of herself. She wondered if nursing might be her true vocation. With a shudder she realised that was nonsense. Even if she could overcome her distaste for the nitty gritty part of the job, there were sure to be plenty of Charles' in the world who were sick.

The room was still and suddenly oppressive. Holding her breath Meg listened, only the faint whirr and click of the central heating broke the thick silence. The quiet was disturbing. Aware of the lack of noise Meg realised what it was she missed made her more aware of the household noises.

There was absolute silence from the bed. Charles lay utterly still; his eyes were open again. He had stopped breathing though, of that she was certain, before she went to him. Surely the injection could not act so quickly?

There was no answering whisper of breath as she put her face close to his. There was no detectable pulse and no throbbing heart as she slipped her fingers under his pyjama jacket. Was he really dead? If she rang the doctor would he detect a flicker of life and use heroic efforts to save Charles.? That would be unthinkable. Remembering the late night TV films, Meg brought her hand mirror from the dressing table and held it in front of Charles' mouth. There was no misting on the mirror

Charles' face was taking on a curious mottied appearance. It was time to ring the doctor.

The number rang out only briefly, Doctor Bickerdyke sounded loud in Meg's ear asking who was calling. Meg sobbed and gasped down the phone, took a deep breath and gabbled like a child.

"This is Meg Goodricke, doctor I'm sorry to disturb you, you remember you came out this evening to see Charles ... that is ... I mean ... last evening."

"Yes, yes, what is it?"

"Oh, doctor he really is much worse, his, his breathing it's so, I, oh, strange." Strange by its' absence she thought.

"For the last hour he's been breathing so... well ... heavily his face is all pinched. I'm sorry to bother you, it must be very late. I mean early, I just don't know what to do." A dry sob drowned her final words.

"I'm on my way, try to keep calm." A bravely stifled sob and Meg put down the receiver, smiling to herself. Taking the door off the latch and propping it ajar for the doctor, she raced upstairs. There was so much to be done, evidence to remove, the stage to be set for the next act.

Young Doctor Bickerdyke found Meg on the floor on her knees, clutching the hand of her dead husband and sobbing great tears of remorse.

"Oh, doctor, I know he's GONE." She could hear the capital letters strident in her voice. The young man was not without a heart, although he had seen it all before.

"Meg come away you can do nothing now. I'm sure it would have made no difference if I had hospitalised Charles." His deft hands were running over the lifeless body, making certain that all life was extinct.

"But why doctor, why did Charles have to die?" It sounded trite and like the dialogue from a second rate film. The doctor seemed not to notice.

"His heart could not stand the strain, there is no doubt in my mind that Charles had a coronary. A heart attack," he kindly interpreted for Meg's benefit. She sighed and buried her head in her hands, mostly to hide the smile of relief that the arrogant young fool was so sure of his diagnosis.

"Take this, it will help you a little." Meg dutifully swallowed the tablet he offered and allowed him to lead her downstairs.

Chapter 19

OPENING her eyes slowly and looking round, Meg found herself lying on the settee, there was a rug across her. Her astonished eyes met those of Gilbert Crabtree who was sitting in Charles' big armchair. He smiled vaguely at her but said nothing.

"Whatever are you doing here?" It sounded so rude but was the first thing that came into her head.

"I've been here a couple of hours."

"But why?"

"Doctor Bickerdyke rang me. He often does you know, in these sort of circumstances". He waved an arm in an embarrassed gesture, his eyes were a clear unusual grey. Perhaps that was what gave his sister Grace her ethereal appearance. Meg realised that he was there in his official capacity as leader of his church flock.

"What happened Margaret, tell me?" The calm serenity of the man, his seductive voice was enough to make anyone confide in him. Meg saw another side to him, to a Gilbert Crabtree she did not know. The urge to babble and pour it all out was overwhelming. There was a great danger beckoning from this man's quiet manner.

"Charles just died, quite suddenly. I mean, I know he was ill but I never dreamed... Oh it's too dreadful." Burying her face in her hands, Meg allowed a couple of shuddering sobs to escape. Gilbert removed her hands into both of his and stared into her dry eyes.

"Tell me exactly what happened. The doctor left yesterday evening and then what happened?" he prompted.

"I don't remember too well, it's all such a nightmare." Her whole body shook, tearing wracking, sobs came from her throat.

"Margaret, that cuts no ice with me," the voice had a note of quiet determination. "What happened?"

"I can't remember, it was terrible," she wailed loudly and flung herself on the floor. Gilbert picked her up and threw her, not very gently, onto the settee and slapped both sides of her face methodically. Leaving her gasping with the shock of his treatment, Gilbert went into the kitchen. She could hear him filling the kettle at the sink. Her indignation quickly died and fear took its' place. What did he know? She realised that he was a force to be reckoned with.

Where was the mild and gentle creature, who stood up each Sunday morning, gripped the edge of the pulpit until his knuckles shone white and urged them all to 'love thy neighbour as thyself'. His sermons always had similar themes.

Meg lit one of her rare cigarettes and was half way through it before Gilbert appeared carrying a tray. He poured tea, put a spoonful of sugar in it, without asking her preference. He sat, again in Charles' armchair and stirred his tea, thoughtfully and for what seemed an unnecessarily long time.

"That's Charles' chair," she said childishly.

"He doesn't need it," laconically from the priest.

"He'll never sit in it again," her lip quivered.

Catching his eye, she quelled the quiver with a hard bite on her lip which brought genuine tears to her eyes.

"For goodness sake, stop staring so," she snapped. "Why are you so interested in what happened to Charles anyway?"

"He was one of my parishioners, he was a fellow human being, but, most of all, he was a friend. I shall miss him greatly." To her intense surprise Meg saw that there were tears in Gilberts' eyes.

"I'm sorry," she muttered ungraciously.

"What is it you're sorry for Margaret, have you something to be ashamed of?"

"No." He really was the most persistent man. "No, I just hadn't realised that you and Charles were such good friends."

The silence dragged on, Gilbert poured himself another cup of tea. Meg waved him away as he offered to take her cup. The lull in the conversation was becoming tense. Whenever she looked up she found the steady grey eyes of the vicar levelled at her. When he finally spoke, Meg thought she was going to faint with the shock.

"Margaret we may as well stop pussy-footing about." Where did he get these words from?

"There is no point in not putting our cards on the table." He leaned forward, elbows on knees, looking into her eyes with deep sadness. "I know Gordon."

"Gordon, Gordon who?" she began to bluster immediately. Her head was ringing, was she about to faint?

"Gordon Hawkins we're talking about. I know Gordon and I know you have been seeing him. You have been meeting lately in Sandford." No bloody secrets with you spying about, she thought. All pretence was suddenly gone, her defence barrier down

"Did Charles know?" she whispered. It was important to her; now that it could not matter; that Charles thought well of her at the end.

"It was no part of my duties to hurt Charles, he loved you dearly Margaret, he didn't deserve to be treated so shabbily."

"He didn't know I was there, he took no notice of me." It sounded petulant and silly. Even she could see that there was no justification.

"You know that's not true. Charles thought the world of you, it was enough for him to be near you. He wanted nothing more."

"He bored me." The excuses seemed more and more empty, less and less of a justification for her behaviour.

"Why did you marry him?"

"He was like my father and he had just died when I met Charles." The illogicality of it suddenly struck her as the absolute truth. She had never before examined her motives in marrying Charles but, with Gilbert's questions, she realised she had married for just that reason. He had been a replacement for her beloved father.

Chapter 20

GILBERT sighed, Meg sat, tense waiting for him to spring.

"A poor basis for marriage," reproached Gilbert.

"Yes, I know that now," she agreed. What did he know about Gordon and how had he found out anyway?

"How did you find out about Gordon?"

"We are old friends, we were at university together. We keep in touch casually"

"Did he tell you how we came to meet?" she tossed out carelessly.

"I know about the marriage bureau, certainly. Gordon wrote to them because he needs a wife." That must be one of the most obvious reasons, thought Meg.

"He needs a wife to give him an air of respectability."

"I should have thought being a surgeon was respectable enough."

"Not really, he needs a wife in the background to give him an appearance of normality. In this imperfect world some minority groups are not well tolerated, especially in his position. He sees a wife as a protective front."

"Front for what?" Meg was utterly bewildered. Gilbert looked sadly over the top of his glasses.

"My dear, Gordon is homosexual." Meg burst out laughing.

"Does that matter to anyone anymore that sort of judgemental criticism belongs to generations ago. Anyway, I don't believe you."

"It's quite true," the priest was very calm. "We were more than friends at university. We were lovers."

She opened her mouth, words formed, there was no sound from her. The silence deepened, she closed he mouth on the soundless words.

Gilbert examined his nails as though he were surprised to see them there at the ends of his fingers.

"Christ," was the one word she could manage.

"Quite," he said tightly. "You must break off this relationship, Margaret, you know that it should never have started."

"You're a fine one to preach," she broke out spitefully.

"My relationship with Gordon is long gone and never hurt anyone. Except ourselves," he added quietly.

"If you tell Gordon about Charles, I'll expose you. I'll make sure that all the parish knows."

"I believe you would Margaret, but you see it doesn't matter. My bishop knows about me, is very aware of the scandal it might cause and would just get me another living where I was not known. In the way the Catholic church moves the paedophile priests. Perhaps it's time for a move anyway. You, however, have no choice. You must not see Gordon again." Meg, who had never done anything she was bidden to do since she was seven years old, nodded in agreement. Gilbert stood up and put his hand on her head murmuring a blessing.

"Now then let's get this funeral arranged. I must go and start services soon," he added quickly. With a shock Meg realised it was Sunday.

Meg made a lovely widow. Black suited her well and she wore a very fetching veil quite in keeping with the best midnight films she watched. She knew it was a bit old fashioned but thought she would be forgiven in the circumstances. She stumbled up the church steps in a convincing way, as though blinded by grief. Roger Benson, from Charles' office, the man always in a muddle with his work, was the one who caught her very expertly and decided he would take charge of her.

"I'll stay with you at the graveside," he whispered in her ear.

"We're going to the crematorium," she hissed back. The decision about cremation had been Meg's. She was adamant when challenged by Gilbert. She had her own very definite reasons but she insisted that it was Charles' wish. Meg had seen enough detective films to know that it was too easy to exhume a body if some amateur detective thought it necessary. She wanted Charles' body out of the way, not lying around waiting for someone to dig it up again.

Doctor Bickerdyke had phoned her and explained, apologetically, that one of his colleagues must see Charles before a cremation certificate could be granted.

"A formality only," he explained in an embarrassed way. "A mere formality," he added for emphasis.

Another doctor had come, shaken Meg by the hand, said nothing and bounded upstairs two at a time. He spent longer in the bathroom washing his hands than he spent in the bedroom. He came down stairs two at a time, shook Meg's hand again and went out of the door as though a tribe of dervish were following him.

Gilbert Crabtree had made a speech about what a fine man Charles had been, how sadly he would be missed, what a loss he would be to the community and how dreadful that he should be taken so young from his grieving widow. It was trite, Gilbert had tears in his eyes, the choir boys looked suitably crestfallen. Meg was moved. The cremation service was rather an anticlimax but Meg felt she had wrung as much as she could from the funeral service long before the curtains closed reverently on Charles' coffin.

Chapter 21

THE mourners had gone, replete with drinks and sandwiches provide by Binny Parsons, the retired nurse who lived opposite. Binny had come into the house while they were at church and, like a fairy godmother, had waved a magic wand over the dusty house.

As the door closed on Roger Benson, who had insisted on being the last to go, a watery winter sun filtered through the windows. Meg saw it as an omen, a promise of better things to come.

The afternoon dragged and Meg began to go through Charles' desk making little piles of papers and documents. The phone rang several times, distant relatives and acquaintances all apologising for not being at the funeral. Such complicated reasons they had too, as though they were trying to get out of a school games lesson on a rainy day, she thought. They all enquired, in hushed tones, if they could do any thing for her. Meg felt they would one and all begin another round of excuses if she did ask for help. The squirrel in Charles had ben responsible for him saving anything and everything. Rubbish and valuables were mixed together, not untidily though, for untidiness had not been his nature. It was a seeming hotch potch of unrelated things. A bank deposit book, building society book and a bundle of national savings certificates were all together in an elastic band. Meg opened them, totted them up and whistled.

That Charles had ben a careful man had been obvious from the early days of their marriage. How careful was now plain to see. Charles had been, in Forsythe speak, a very warm man indeed. His widow would not have to worry about having to go out to earn a crust.

"Thank you dear," she addressed the photo of Charles on the comer of the desk.

"Thank you very much," she added as she found the mortgage protection plan. The house was now hers with no further repayments to make now that Charles could not do so.

"You shouldn't spoil me so," she said coyly when she found a bundle of premium bonds. Charles smiled as she blew him a kiss.

"You are a darling," she purred when she rediscovered the locket and pendant she had come across a few days previously.

With sudden resolution she decided to sell Charles' Volvo. It was too big for her and she had her own car. The Volvo would go for a good price. The local paper agreed to run an advert in their used-car columns. For two nights she said, when the clerk asked and she agreed to put a cheque in the post. Fearful of Gilberts' reaction she decided that discretion would be the best policy as far as Gordon was concerned. That she had made a promise to Gilbert did not weigh heavily, she just didn't want to be found out breaking the promise.

She had written Gordon a brief note, mentioning neither Charles nor Gilbert, but made it plain that their association was at an end.

She had no real regrets, he had been a rather opinionated companion and the prospect of a mutually celibate life with Gordon; the vicar like a shadow in the background; did not appeal to Meg. She had reached that time of middle life when madness attacks some people and excitement becomes more important than the security they have striven for over the previous years.

There was this rising excitement, an inner restlessness in Meg. She felt that a chapter in her life had now closed and there must be better things to come. Certainly to confine herself to a quiet life and widowhood was not in her nature. There was a certain status attendant on widowhood. She could become a scion of the local community, a pillar of the church. But only part-time she vowed, only when the world observed her. When unobserved her private life would be very private indeed.

Binny Parsons rang the bell and opened the door in one smooth movement. "Tea time," she called over her shoulder as she disappeared into the kitchen. Useless to protest that a stiff brandy was more on the lines that Meg was thinking along. Smiling wanly at Binny, Meg dutifully drank the mahogany coloured tea which tasted of tarmacadam and ate the only slightly burnt toast. The boiled egg she refused absolutely to touch, despite obvious disappointment from her neighbour. Binny left soon after six and promised to call again tomorrow. She assured Meg that things would look brighter then.

Meg felt things were already much brighter in view of Charles financial standing. A long period of mourning was not for her and she was already thinking of holidays. Remembering Sven and the way he spoke so enthusiastically about his home, she determined to ask for more details. She put a reassuring note through Binny's door and set off for the meeting with Sven.

Chapter 22

HE was waiting in 'their' cafe, both hands cupping a large mug and gazing into its' depths as though seeking the answer to the mysteries of life itself. His face had the vulnerable look she had noticed on their first meeting. His shoulders slumped dejectedly.

Leaping up as she approached the table, he grasped both her hands in his. She had the idea that his smile would meet somewhere round the back of his neck.

"I had thought you were not coming, that something had happened to keep you." Not wild horses nor dead husbands, she thought. "So much have I missed you," he buried his nose down her ear.

Reluctantly unhanding him she sat and drank thirstily from his pale eyes, seeking there some clue as to the magnetism of the man.

"You have had quiet week?"

"Deadly," smiling warmly at him.

"I had to attend the inquest of the grocer, I told you about him. Do you remember?"

"Vaguely."

"They went over every detail of his life."

"Every detail?" she panicked.

"You do not want to hear do you?"

"Not really." The faint fluttering bird within her chest had become a great eagle with thumping, beating wings.

"What was the verdict?" she croaked as the giant bird blocked off her windpipe.

"Oh, it was an accident of course, no-one would deliberately kill themselves in that way."

"Of course not," she laughed shrilly.

"There was nothing to suggest that anyone else had been there. Nothing to hint that he had been pushed onto the bacon machine." Her laughter sounded maniacal in her ears.

"An accident, poor Charles." Poor Charles indeed and for the second time she didn't know which Charles she sighed for.

"The sauna, yes? You would like to go?". He was like a child begging a treat.

"I'd love to" , she said, rewarding him.

"Come," he leapt up grasped her hand and rushed headlong for the door. Meg just had time to snatch up her mac. Only just.

His car must have been one of those that went from nought to ninety in three seconds she thought, as they roared across the town and zipped onto the motorway. Barely daring to breathe she would not have dreamed of speaking. Half a ton of gravel rearranged itself as they slewed to a halt at the sauna club steps.

"This time you must go in the cold plunge". She peered through the November gloom at the frost-encrusted shrubbery and raised her eyebrows.

"Of course, last time you went only in the small cold plunge, not in the pool with the ice blocks. You will enjoy it."

"Lovely." Her nipples ached, her varicosed vein throbbed. This time Sven was ready before her. She came, naked and shivering, into the hot house to find him sitting, cross legged, finger tips together and eyes closed. She watched him for a while, not caring to interrupt his communion with God.

"Sven," she whispered for fear that God would be cross at the interruption. "Sven," louder this time.

"Ohmmm." she felt she had misheard and waited. The word was repeated several more times before she shook his shoulder. The pale eyes came back into focus from some far fields of Valhalla.

"It is Trancendental Meditation. Twice a day for twenty minutes I practice this. It helps me to relax and keep control of myself." Please don't do that she wanted to yell, I don't mind you losing control of yourself. "Self-discipline is very important."

"And the Ohmmm?"

"It is my mantra." How foolish of me she commented. Meg found the sauna less exhausting this time. Perhaps, she thought, it's like toothache, you get used to the dull throb of pain. The iced pool she found too painful to think about.

"It is all in your mind you know. You are not really cold, you only think that you are." Sven was cheerful. His body glowed ruddily all over. Absolutely everywhere.

"I'm sure you're right," said Meg as she looked at the blue discolouration of her feet with considerable interest.

The purple and white mottling on her hands and arms she found most unattractive. Wrapping the big turkish towel about her Meg buried her face in the luxury and warmth of it.

"No, no you must rub hard, so." The first comfort she had felt that day was rudely snatched away and Sven began to towel her roughly. Meg felt an acre of skin lift from her back. The rough pummeling continued. I shall have third degree burns in a moment, she thought.

The scrubbing stopped and Sven began running up and down on the spot. God, she thought, he's beautiful. Faster, faster went Sven, legs up and down like pistons, his knees touching his belly each time. It's so unfair wailed Meg to herself, why is he so unaware of the effect he has on me. Surely he can hear this pounding in my chest, this roaring in my ears.

"You feel good yes?"

"Yes, it's good." she thought of her dentist with affection who always anaesthetised her before he set the drill going.

Meg dressed as rapidly as her frozen fingers would allow. It was sheer will-power and a desperate need to conserve every last therm of body heat that made her able to force buttons through holes.

"Irish coffee," she said firmly as she settled herself at the hotel bar. "Iced orange juice," he ordered. Meg wondered of it could be fanaticism with him or a fetish. Weird religion maybe?

"Do you skate?" His smile would have melted a heart of stone. Meg warmed herself on it and considered the question. At about the age of eight she had been the champion roller skater of Harbour Yard. She suspected that Sven did not mean that.

"I mean ice skating," he said, doing his mind reading act.

"No, no I cannot skate."

"Then I will teach you," he was triumphant. "You will not fall, I will hold you." The sounded nice, but where? "It will be at the rink of course. There is one in Wasterburn. We will go next week yes? You must wear warm clothes, it is very cold on the ice. Very cold."

It bloody would be, she thought. Why could they not go somewhere warm for once and just be still. Meg felt an aching nostalgia for the fuggy little pubs she used to go to with Eliot. Eliot had been long before Charles, in the distant days when she had done just as she liked and to hell with the rest of the world.

"You are day dreaming. Will you come to the rink? It is fun," he added by way of inducement. By whose criteria she wondered.

They agreed to meet at their usual place next Monday. A detached corner of her mind tried desperately to analyse her motives. Sven was obviously gorgeous and good company, if you liked being cold. But where was it all leading, were they destined to leap from one frantic activity to another like a couple of ten year olds? Although completely unable to fathom it she agreed to the next meeting.

Chapter 23

TURNING the car into the driveway, she thought she saw the curtain twitch at Binny Parsons house. Sod her, why shouldn't I go out? I'm not neglecting a house full of children. There was no neighbourly visit that evening and Meg made hot tea and promised herself a hot bath later.

Noting that the salt cellars round her neck were deeper than usual, she continued undressing and then stood naked on the bathroom scales. Mournfully noting that she'd lost half a stone in the past week, she sighed. Peering in the mirror she saw that her nose was very much thinner, witch-like she decided as she pulled the covers around her aching body.

Meg dragged herself to the door in answer to the bell. Who on earth could be visiting at this time of day.? It was still dark outside.

"Good morning," shouted Binny Parsons as she swept past Meg and through into the kitchen. "I knew you were up. Saw your lights," she added as though to dispel the idea that she was clairvoyant.

"What time is it," whispered Meg as she watched Binny, horror struck.

"Half past seven. I'm doing you a nice omelette for breakfast. We must have some good sound packing to get through the day."

"I never eat breakfast."

"There you are then," said Binny enigmatically. The omelette was shaken, folded and slid deftly onto a plate.

"Put yourself round that, it will stick your ribs together." Meg was not sure this was an attractive prospect.

"Oh, Binny I really can't. There's much too much. Perhaps if you shared it?"

"Wouldn't hear of it. Had mine at six ack- emma. Come along, get stuck in." Meg trailed the fork in a desultory way around the plate, fighting the rising nausea.

"I see you came in late last night." Binny had a knowing leer sat tight on her face. Oh God, the egg is coming back thought Meg as her heart stopped for an aching two seconds.

"Yes I couldn't bear the house any longer, the emptiness, you know..." she trailed off

"I went for a long drive. Don't really know where I went just about ..." she finished lamely smiling wanly into Binny's curious eyes.

"Shock." Binny nodded to emphasise her diagnosis and poured Meg another cup of tea. It had the consistency of beef stew.

"I much prefer coffee," she was apologetic.

"Yes, but not to start the day. That's a continental habit," she hissed. Early morning coffee was obviously the height of depravity. "The first six weeks are worst after..." The word hung in the air. Why was everyone reluctant to say the word death? It was apparently the forbidden topic now. Sex, drugs and venereal diseases were discussed over the dinner table with children. The really taboo topic is death.

"After Daddy …went, I was in a sort of fog, went about not knowing what was going on. It was only Mr. Micawber who kept me sane." Meg remembered that this was Binny's golden retriever. Obviously, Freud-trained in psychotherapy.

"Of course, before Daddy…Mr. Micawber and he were inseparable. He turned to me in our common loss. Best of pals we've been since Daddy…" Time in Binny's life was divide into pre-Daddy and post Daddy phases. Before Christ and after Christ

"What did your father die of?"

"Bee stings."

"I'm sorry?"

"Mr. Micawber turned over a hive and Daddy tried to pull him off but the bees just turned on him. Not many stings. Daddy allergic. Went very quickly in the end." Meg cast around for some way to distract Binny from what was a very distressing topic.

"I've eaten most of your lovely omelette," in her good-little-girl voice.

"Good, now you're ready for anything." For what, thought Meg as the endless day stretched ahead.

"I must write some letters," she said in a kindly attempt to get rid of Binny. Binny had other ideas and insisted on clearing away the pots and washing up.

"I'm sorry," she said, showing Meg a tea cup in one hand, the handle in the other.

"It really doesn't matter," and it didn't. Meg could buy some more. That's it. I can go on a spending spree.

Chapter 24

MEG wrote the bread-and-butter letters that were owing to those who had sent sympathy notes. They mostly wanted a blow by blow account of how Charles had died. She would give them a suitably edited version.

Haynes and Hill, the big store on Silver Street had just the tea set she wanted. There were large red poppies on the cups and tumbling green leaves on the saucers. Just the sort of thing Charles would have labelled vulgar. Meg liked it because it was jolly.

"Shall I wrap it now or can we send it Mrs. Goodricke?" Gazing blankly at the assistant Meg wondered how she knew her name.

"Perhaps you could send it. I'm going upstairs for some other things."

"Tell the assistant about this and we can send them all together." The picture department had a violent sea scape which she took to immediately. The fawning young man said he would send it no problem, he knew the address. Wandering into Pottleton's book store she chose a couple of thrillers and an expensive book with lovely illustrations of garden flowers.

A pub lunch seemed a good idea but first she would throw the books into the car. A young constable was wandering along the row of parked cars, making an occasional note in his copy book.

"Have I overstayed my welcome officer?"

"No, Mrs Goodricke, you're alright here for two hours. Some people aren't though." He grinned as he slapped a ticket on the nearby car.

How does everyone know my name? Suddenly the whole town knew her and yet she did not remember ever having been addressed by name before although Charles sometimes was when they were out together. Had been, had been, remembering to make him in the past tense.

The whole town seemed to be spying on her. Feeling ill tempered and persecuted she ground up the gears savagely and roared off. Dammit, she would get out of this pokey town. Suddenly deciding to make for Wasterburn she turned left without signalling. Waving gaily at the driver behind who had to leap on his brakes, she put her foot down.

It was market day when she got there and she had some difficulty parking. She found a pub car park, limited to customers only. The choice having been made for her she pushed open the door of the lounge bar. The place was full of farmers in tweed jackets and loud voices.

Wading her way through a farmer-sized meat pie she looked up to see a man opposite gazing at her. She picked up her brandy glass. He watched her throat contract as she swallowed. Meg nibbled round the crust of her pie. Grey tweed jacket monitored every movement. The course of another gulp of brandy was followed as far as her navel. Meg thought he must be one of the army of people who seemed to know her today.

"Do you know me?"

"No ma'am, but I would very much like to." His bold gaze scoured round her face and locked onto her eyes. He gave a sudden nervous grin and Meg felt her irritation with the day vanish. He stood up slowly and was standing for ever. Looking him up and down Meg estimated him at six feet four or five. His back, as he stood at the bar, must have been eight feet across. Lovely, she thought, wriggling in her seat.

"How did you know what I was drinking?" She looked at the glass he put in front of her.

"I heard you at the bar when I came in." So, he had been watching her for some time.

"Thank you," she took a drink. Again he watched her throat. "It's like the snake and the mongoose."

"I'm not a snake, I'm Allan."

"Hello Allan I'm Meg." Why she had given her real name she did not know. It was entirely against her nature to be honest with anyone unless it were unavoidable. Draining his glass in one swallow Allen stood.

"Come on let's get out of here." Meg grabbed her coat and followed meakly. Allen what? She wondered.

The pub car park was bitterly cold after the steamy meat-pie warmth of the bar. Allen helped her into her coat, his hands lingering an unnecessarily long time on her shoulders.

"Will you come home with me? I have a car here but it's not far."

"I have my own," indicating her vehicle.

Eyeing him up and down Meg decided that he was really very attractive. It was tempting but did she want the involvement? It was foolish to pass up the chance now after weeks of seeking such an encounter.

Allan pulled a big Citreon recklessly out of the car park and shot up the road. At the traffic lights Meg saw that they had pulled up outside a church. St. Stephen's, she read on the notice board. This was the name of Gilbert Crabtree's church. Thinking of Gilbert, she saw his reproachful eyes staring at her through the windscreen. A sudden realisation came to her. What was she doing picking up a stranger and offering to go home with him. She did not think Allan was taking her home to show her his garden.

Looking far ahead she saw that his car was some distance ahead. With instant resolution Meg turned left, breathed a deep sigh as though she had been released from an ordeal, she turned east on the by-pass and headed to Castlebridge.

Chapter 25

SHE saw the man standing on the doorstep as she turned the car into the gateway. He opened the car door and took her parcels.

"Sam Piggott," he thrust his hand out and enclosed hers entirely. Meg introduced herself and pulled her hand away. It felt crushed and looked white. Leading him into the living room, she turned on the table lamp and wall light above Charles' Dutch interiors. The resultant glow she thought rather romantic.

"I must tell you I want the top price for the car. It's in excellent condition. My husband was a careful man" she added as though this would enhance the price.

"I'm sure that he was, but I haven't come about the car." Meg gazed blankly at him and waited for his explanation. The car was the only reason she could think of for him to be there.

"My name is Detective Inspector Sam Piggott." A bucket of icy water was thrown down Meg's spine and a firm hand gripped her throat. Putting a hand up to lose the choking fingers, she tried speech. A strangled 'oh' was wrenched from her.

"I'm stationed with the Chester Criminal Investigation Department." He said as though it might make him more acceptable to Meg. She did not feel that it did.

"I'm investigating the death of Charles Rogerson." Oh, him, thought Meg , that was nothing to do with her. Her guilty conscience had immediately projected images of her dead murdered husband.

"I believe you knew Mr. Rogerson?" It was not really a question.

"Charles Rogerson?" she gasped.

"The grocer who died two weeks ago in rather distressing circumstances."

"I read something about it." Every avid detail but she was not going to tell this man a thing.

"You did know him." The flat statement sounded menacing.

"Should I have known him?" Although the constant hedging and parrying were to give her time, she still could not think what to do. Could she deny all knowledge of him, or admit that she knew him but had not seen him on the day that he died?

"I didn't know him." She looked straight at the inspector in what she imagined to be a thoroughly honest way. He sighed and shook his head slowly.

"Oh dear Mrs. Goodricke, don't make it difficult for me." Tough, she thought, my heart bleeds for you but I'm dammed if I will tell you anything.

"I seem to remember that I read an inquest on the man?" Her puzzled expression was quite genuine. "Surely inquests put an end to things. Over and done with, loose ends tied up?" she shut up abruptly, realising that she was elaborating too much. The inspector weighed up her little speech, nodding his head to give his deliberation its' due.

"That is true, generally speaking. Sometimes however, we come across new evidence." Meg felt the room spinning.

"New evidence would put a different complexion on things. New evidence would mean we would have to investigate further. Widen our net," he added. Net had a definite menacing cadence to it. Although his speech was slow and measured, his manner considerate, Meg did not for a moment suppose him to be a fool.

"New evidence?" Repeating that awful word yet again.

"I'm not at liberty to disclose information," he said primly. "We do know that you had been seeing him. His diary was pretty explicit about your relationship."

"Relationship! Relationship what relationship? I did not know the man." Her voice had risen to a crescendo. Inspector Piggott shook his head wonderingly. He waited patiently as though expecting Meg to lie on the carpet and kick in a tantrum. Thinking the danger period over, he cleared his throat.

"Charles Rogerson left a diary. Your telephone number was in it. The name was wrong but the number and description tallied." He was patient in his explanation as if it were important to him that she understood his viewpoint. "You had an appointment to meet him on the day he died. What happened Mrs. Goodricke?"

"I didn't see him that day. I mean, he didn't turn up." She was gabbling, her explanations were the invention of the moment.

"Ahh," along drawn out sigh. "You did know him then." Sod it I fell for that. Meg bit her lip in frustration, she hoped the pain would sharpen her wits.

"We met casually. Once."

"Charles Rogerson's diary describes a more explicit relationship than one meeting would give rise to. He described quite a torrid love affair. In great detail," he added slowly savouring every word.

"I don't care what crap he wrote, it just isn't true." Her voice was strident, she was really rattled.

"Would you care to explain the entries in his diary then?"

"No I wouldn't." Her teeth snapped together decisively. How could she be held responsible for the sexual fantasies of a stranger. Her resentment towards Charles Rogerson knew no bounds. How dare he weave this web of untrue romance about her? Meg felt she was the only one with a franchise on untruths.

Chapter 26

"YOU must have known him some considerable time." It was a flat statement, not a question. Meg felt a splash of cold fear around her feet which crept up her ankles. She lit one cigarette from the end of another, poured a large brandy and tried to quell the panic within her.

Sam Piggott had gone with a cheery wave, a hope that she would get her price for the car and a promise to return again. Meg found no comfort in the fact that he had not arrested her there and then. The inspector had said he would give her time to think things over in the light of the information she had given him. It was more likely, she thought, it was to consult with his senior officers.

The second brandy made things look a little less bleak. Contemplating refilling her glass, she was aware of a shadow across the kitchen window.

"Yoo hoo," the powerful voice of Binny Parsons was unmistakable. "I saw you had a visitor so I waited until he had gone." Binny looked enquiringly at Meg.

"He came to ask about Charles' car," said Meg obligingly.

"You haven't sold it?" Binny sounded really alarmed.

"No, he wouldn't meet my offer."

"I do know the vicar was very interested. I wonder he hasn't been round to see you. For goodness sake don't agree to a part exchange," she guffawed. Meg smiled at the thought of the old Morris eight that Gilbert Crabtree tootled around in. It had running boards it was so old.

Binny was eyeing the brandy bottle and the brimming ash-tray.

"This is no way to get into, you ought to keep occupied, take your mind off things. And eat proper meals. Come to me this evening, I'll cook for us both and it will be company for you. I usually watch television until about ten. Television had no interest for Meg. An evening listening to childish laughter from Binny did not appeal.

"Binny I'm terribly sorry but I must go out. I have to go to Sandford. To see an old aunt of Charles'." Aunts were very convenient people to have in the background. Not for the first time she regretted her lack of them.

"Have a nice nap then before you go." Binny eyed the brandy bottle again obviously showing great restraint in not adding that Meg ought to sleep it off. With her usual earth-shattering slam of the door, Binny was gone. The brandy caught up with the lunch time drinks and the idea of sleep became overwhelming, Meg stretched out on the settee.

Struggling up from a dream about escaping from Devil's Island, she realised it was the door bell which had roused her. She was surprised to see, by the hall clock, that her incarceration on the island had taken three hours.

"I saw the car and realised you were in," said Gilbert Crabtree, pushing rather rudely past Meg. He had the grace to wait while she invited him into the living room.

"Why didn't you tell me you were selling Charles 'car." His voice was accusing as though she had deliberately set out to deceive.

"Didn't know that you were interested," her tone was soothing and quiet to calm Gilbert's nerves. "Binny just told me, it would have saved the ad if you had declared your interest sooner."

"I hadn't thought you would be selling so soon." His manner was calmer but his attitude seemed one of embarrassment.

"Do you want to buy Gilbert?"

"Well actually yes," his discomfort was more obvious. "The fact is I do want the car but I can't afford it just now." He glowered at Meg as though his financial problems were of her making. "I can give you half now and half at the end of the month. I'm assuming you want the book price?"

"You know how well it was looked after."

"I do, it will be worth every penny. I just don't have the cash until my salary goes into the bank at the month end." Meg found it rather strange to hear a vicar talking about his salary as though he were a bank clerk or a school teacher. It made him less ascetic. She wondered what he spent his money on when he wasn't buying cars. She imagined his few pleasures as being rather pathetic. In which case she could afford to be magnanimous.

"Take the car if you want it Gilbert. After all I can't drive two cars and it's only stuck in the garage. Pay me when you can. I'm not going anywhere." Jesus, I hope not, remembering Sam Piggott.

"Will a post-dated cheque be O.K?"

"Yes, of course. Take the dammed car." Meg was impatient with Gilbert and his nonsense.

"How are you feeling Margaret?" His changing tack suddenly disconcerted Meg.

"I'm alright, a bit lost yet but coping. I wrote to Gordon." She felt that putting it right now would in some way justify the original relationship.

"I know, Gordon rang me. He was disappointed and wanted to take it further. I advised him to drop it and take your letter as final. You won't hear from him again," he added confidently.

"He wasn't the only man I was seeing, there was another." She concentrated on Charles Rogerson and conveniently forgot Sven. Gilbert made no comment, his mouth twitched fractionally.

"He died, this other man I mean, he died and the police came to see me about it," she added in a rush of confidence.

"What had it to do with you?"

"Nothing, absolutely nothing. It was pure chance he died on the day I was supposed to be meeting him. But I didn't, see him, he didn't turn up." she was beginning to feel that, if she repeated the story often enough, it would become second nature. Might even become as she wanted it to be rather than as it was.

"You were not involved in any way in the man's death Margaret?"

"No, not at all. Gazing deep into Gilbert's eyes she willed him to believe her.

"Then you have nothing to fear."

Chapter 27

DESPITE Gilbert's logical; but she felt far too trusting; assumption, Meg was not reassured.

Taking her car out after Gilbert had gone, she set off for Sandford. The town looked dreary and lifeless. Eventually she had to settle for seeing a film at The Grand. Meg found it only slightly better than watching T.V. with Binny.

Going home she thought how ridiculous it was that she should go to the next town to see a film. What was so wicked about doing something so simple only a week after a family death? It must matter to her what other people thought more than she knew. Castlebridge looked deserted as though everyone was sitting round their own fireplaces. Snug and sleepy with their families about them. Meg felt a wave of desolation and loneliness engulf her. She was not jealous of cosy suburbia, that was, after all, what she was trying to escape. Her longing for excitement and travel was where her thoughts were centred. Meg had the idea that perhaps her longings might find their realisation through Sven. On the whole, she reflected, she was not getting very far with him. His urgent need to punish his body to the point of exhaustion was incomprehensible to her.

Melancholy with her sad evening and restless with unfulfilled passion, she searched the bathroom cupboard for a sleeping pill. With venomous thoughts of Charles she remembered that he had swallowed them all. That he had not been consulted on the matter she did not find any less selfish of him.

After an uneasy sleep had finally overtaken her, Meg woke with a blinding headache. Feeling murderous toward Binny, she went to open the door. It was Inspector Sam Piggott standing on the doorstep. Opening the door wider Meg saw another, younger, man with him. The young man was leaning against the wall, crushing the winter jasmine and picking the spots on his chin.

"Good morning!" Sam Piggott had obviously risen early, breakfasted well and all was right in his world. "This is my sergeant Harry Lake" Meg had not realised that inspectors had personal sergeants. The man nodded, shifted his gum from one cheek to the other and held out his hand. Having seen the spot picking session Meg pretended not to see the hand. Shrugging, Harry Lake returned to his absorbing hobby. He wore a hat which she found unusual in a young man. It was tipped over his eyes and gave him a rather sinister look. He would have been pleased that Meg thought him sinister. It was a look he tried to foster. Harry watched a lot of detective films.

"You were out last evening." a bland statement from Inspector Piggott.

"Yes I went to Sandford." She didn't see there was any reason she should not go out if she wished. It struck her like a thunderbolt that perhaps the police were following her. She dismissed it as too absurd and dramatic.

"We saw you go out and return." Harry Lake had an americanised accent, a long drawl in his speech. It was carefully cultivated. Inspector Piggott silenced him with a glare.

'Meg was silent but invited them both in with a gesture. Sergeant Lake made no attempt to remove his Humphrey Bogart hat until Sam gazed very pointedly at his head.

"Mrs. Goodricke have you thought about our conversation of yesterday afternoon?"

"Not really. Was there any reason why I should?" The inspector sighed.

"I wondered if there was anything you wanted to add to what you told me. I advise you to tell the truth about Charles Rogerson."

"You did and I did." This did not sound so cool as she had hoped.

"Might I remind you of the diary Mr. Rogerson kept. He was very detailed about your relationship."

"I have already said that there was no relationship and whatever the man wrote about me is not true. I do not know why I should be subjected to someone else's fantasies."

"Do you have an overcoat Mrs. Goodricke?"

"Several, why?"

"Do you have a green one?" The morning sun was suddenly shut out as Meg denied having one.

"I would have thought it an obvious choice- a green coat for a woman of your colouring?"

"My husband didn't like green, he thought it unlucky." Meg was desperately casting around for some way out of the conversation.

"Would you like some coffee?"

"No, thank you we have a lot to do today." The inspector smiled his tolerant smile and got up.

"Mrs. Goodricke I would advise you against planning on going away anywhere. You have a passport do you?"

"Yes why?"

"We would like you to keep yourself available for questioning." His smile was back but it did not reach so far across his face this time.

"This is monstrous. What do you suspect me of? I did not know this Rogerson man and I certainly had nothing to do with his death."

"Then you have nothing to fear from telling the truth." This time the smile barely touched his cheek. Shades of Gilbert in that expression.

Locking the door, turning off the light and pouring herself a beaker of coffee Meg sat in the corner of the room on the floor. She was out of sight of the window. The doorbell which heralded the arrival of Binny went unheeded. Sod her she thought as she settled down to think about her situation. Binny is the last person to confide in. Sitting on the floor, back to the wall with her first two fingers in her mouth Meg gazed about the room. It was her posture in times of extreme stress, that of a cornered animal. On the couple of occasions when he had been witness to this primitive behaviour Charles had been amused. He had laughed and said that if a car had sped through the room she would be unable to avoid it – like a rabbit caught in the headlights. When he had seen that it was not for effect or for attention he had been very kind, had picked her up, removed the soggy fingers and cuddled her. Sometimes, she thought, a tear of self-pity escaping down her cheek, Charles had been a darling.

Chapter 28

THE tensions Meg felt began slowly to unknot as she rhythmically chewed on her fingers. Her uppermost worry was about the overcoat. Had the inspector found her green coat? How? It could not have just been a casual remark he made. It must be that he had the coat but could not establish that it was hers. Anyway, if he had it there was no reason to panic. It had been cleaned. Meg was uncertain whether blood stains could be left after dry cleaning. At all costs she must stick to the story about the nose bleed which she had told the woman in the dry cleaners.

The door chimes broke through her reverie and Meg had the feeling that they had been sounding for some time. Gilbert Crabtree stood on the step.

"Margaret why did you not answer? Binny rang me to say you were in but were not answering the door. She was worried."

"I was only having a bath," she said wearily. Why all the panic because she wanted to be alone?

"Why the panic?. I'm not a child." Gilbert looked at her hunted eyes and pushed her into the living-room.

"Whatever it is, you look dreadful."

"I'm alright, Gilbert. I just don't feel very sociable."

"Have the police been back again?" He was either very shrewd or a good guesser. Meg gave in.

"They came this morning. Said I must not leave the country." Her voice was high-pitched and uncertain. "Gilbert, I had nothing to do with this man dying. You do believe me don't you?"

"I do actually." He sounded surprised at his own incredulity.

"Well then why doesn't Inspector Piggott believe me?"

"He doesn't know you as I do Margaret. You really need someone who knows you well to convince them. I do not think I am the right person. They would think me prejudiced anyway."

"Who can I ask?"

"What about Tudor Baines. He is your solicitor is he not? If Ted can't help then no-one can." Meg was not sure she cared for Gilbert's turn of phrase. That she might be beyond saving was a sobering enough thought. That she needed a solicitor was another.

"Do you think I need a solicitor?"

"Good grief, no. But it is good to have officialdom on your side. Belt and braces you know. Belt and braces." His use of silly idioms was as irritating as ever, his laugh did not convince Meg. Gilbert looked away when she tried to catch his eye.

"Alright," she was suddenly resolute. "I'll see Mr. Baines. Perhaps he can get these policemen off my back or find out what it is they have against me."

"That's the way, cards on the table, make a clean breast of it all with him. No point in beating about the bush." Meg wondered how many more metaphors he could introduce into the conversation. He bounded to the door, snatched it open and was gone with a loud slam of wood on wood.

Meg could hear him shouting something as he roared away in his old Morris. Another trite remark no doubt. The receptionist put her through at once when she said who was calling.

"It will be a little while until your husbands' estate is settled Mrs. Goodricke," said the voice at the other end of the line. "If you are having any small money problems I can, of course let you have an advance."

"Mr. Baines, it's not money. May I come and see you. Today if possible please."

"Dear lady, yes of course, but I will come to your house. That would be better." Meg had discovered lately that newly bereaved people could expect to be 'grounded' for some time after the funeral meats had been eaten. As though one were not expected to be able to think.

"Very well. This afternoon Mr. Baines." Although he had always seemed to be as old as God, Meg assumed that Tudor Baines was about sixty. His nose had become more hooked, his shoulders more rounded over the years. The comfortable cuddly paunch which Meg remembered had become more defined. The force of gravity was dragging everything downwards. He stood, rubbing his hands together, Uriah Heap fashion. Meg noticed that they were not very clean. His hair looked as though it had last been washed on Friday of Christmas week. You repulsive man shuddered Meg.

"The police think I murdered a man." The hand washing stopped immediately.

"Surely not, dear lady, surely not."

"They keep coming to see me about it, hoping that I'll confess I suppose."

"You told them nothing I hope?" His voice was sharp and his expression changed. Meg thought this strange that his first question was not 'did you do it?'.

"No, I haven't said anything because I didn't do it."

"Quite right, quite right. You should have sent for me sooner. I could have sorted it all out I'm sure."

"Gilbert Crabtree said I should consult you." Was that a flicker of distaste.? But no.

"A sound man, a sound man." He was like a yodeller listening for the mountains to throw his voice back. His hand washing started up with renewed vigour. He leapt back when she offered a cigarette and looked so horrified that she put the box away.

"Tell me the story from the beginning." Meg began her tale and of her meeting with Charles Rogerson (quite by accident) she insisted. She related how she was to have met the grocer that day but that he never turned up. Next day she had read of his death in the local paper. She told the story well, clearly and with conviction.

"Yes, well done. Now tell me the truth dear lady. Tell me the truth." The horrible little turd has not been listening, she thought.

"You haven't been listening."

"Oh I have, to every word. Unfortunately, they are not the true ones."

Chapter 29

TUDOR Baines' scruffy appearance was obviously very deceptive. His mind was a complete contradiction. Meg could almost hear Gilbert Crabtree saying 'the Lord looks not on the outer man'.

The well washed, dried and rubbed hands were pushed deep into the solicitor's pockets.

"When you want to tell me the truth I will listen, or when the police come to interview you again then I will help if you give me a call." He bounced up and down on the balls of his feet and unexpectedly rushed to the front door as though Meg were chasing him. He waited by the door, one foot forward, a runner poised for the starters' gun, while Meg opened the door. He excelled himself as he bounced down the steps.

"The truth, the truth, the truth, goodbye." Looking at the clock she was surprised to see that it was still only mid-afternoon. She felt it ought to be bedtime. Her tea was a beaker of coffee laced with brandy. Her dinner was more of the same. She enjoyed both meals thoroughly. As Meg was draining the last drop of her dinner, the phone rang.

"It's Binny" boomed the childish voice. "I haven't seen you all day and wondered if you would like to come over.

I'm not doing anything special, listening to music and generally lolling about, Do come." Her invitation was warm and delivered in an unusually sensible manner.

"Binny I'd love to come." There was nothing else to say. To have refused would have been too churlish.

"I'll put the garage light on for you. It shines up the path."

Dear Binny, mused Meg, maudlin on an empty stomach and too much brandy. She really is the only friend I have. The door was on the latch and Meg stood in the warm hallway staring at the deer head sprouting from the wall.

"Oh dear," Binnys' trained nurses' eye had taken in Megs' tousled hair crumpled skirt and carpet slippers.

"Forgotten to change your slippers?"

"Certainly not. I thought it wasn't worth changing. It's not miles over the road." She didn't want absent mindedness to be chalked up with her other sins. Binny valiantly did not back away from the brandy fire surrounding Meg.

"I bet you haven't eaten much today. What can I get for you?" Binny was launched on her food- is- the-panacea-for-all-ills, kick.

"Nothing thank you, I'm too full."

"I daresay," drily. "Never mind you're maybe better without. Come and sit where it's warm." She led Meg into an over warm room, settled her into an enormous arm chair. A huge mug of a steamy milk drink was pushed into her hand. It was not familiar to Meg but tasted faintly of malt.

"Drink up. What are your tastes in music?"

"This is lovely," Meg nodded to the stereo. The haunting delicate strains of a flute whispered around the room.

"Chopin, actually," Binny was embarrassed. "I have something more rousing if you would prefer. I know Charles used to like choral music."

Meg looked carefully at Binny. How could she know Charles' taste in music? Did she also know that Meg had not shared those interests?

"I didn't always care for his music but this is beautiful. I could listen to this all evening. Her eyelids were prickly, her lids were heavy.

"Do put your feet up and relax, I won't be offended if you drop off." The laugh was soft, gentle not her usual guffaw. The warmth, the music, the kindness all caught up with Meg. She refused to admit that the beakers of brandy might have contributed to her emotional state. Within a few minutes she was curled in the armchair and un-headed tears were tumbling down her cheeks. Binny let the silent misery take its' course.

"Is it anything I can help with or are you just missing Charles?" Meg gasped, shook her head and gulped. Binny was unable to decide which question was being denied.

"Crying is very therapeutic." this new, sympathetic Binny was a puzzle to Meg. She seemed so much more mature. "I don't act the fool all the time, we all have a front to show the world." Her tone had a touch of bitterness and Meg wondered if the silly appearance Binny usually presented was a way of keeping the world at bay. It was very effective. No-one took Binny seriously.

"Gilbert Crabtree is a great help to me, but I realise he is not everyone's cup of tea."

"Gilbert?"

"Yes, he's a tower of strength if you're in real need. He has spent hours talking to me when I've wanted to kill myself."

Meg gaped at this new Binny. There was nothing she could say that would not sound trite and superficial.

"Have you ever felt the need to self-destruction?" Binny said it as though such feelings were like indigestion, more of a nuisance than anything else, Meg had never felt such an impulse, but was certainly familiar with the other side of the coin. The urge to destroy others.

"The police think I killed a man, Binny. I didn't but they think they have evidence against me."

"Yes I know, you must be very worried. Gilbert told me. He said you knew the man who died."

"Gilbert Crabtree told you about me?", her voice was incredulous. How could he gossip in this way, She had told him about the police visit in confidence? She snapped crossly at Binny.

"He had no right to tell you about it."

"My dear, Gillbert is the biggest gossip I know. He is completely unable to hold his own water. I very much doubt if he could ever keep a secret."

Chapter 30

IT was late when Meg finally went home. She had discussed her situation with Binny who had been sensible with her advice and taken Tudor Baines attitude that it was better to admit nothing to the police.

"The onus," Binny had pointed out, "was on them to prove their case." Crossing the road home Meg felt sure she saw a bulky shadow under the neighbour's laburnum tree move, as though someone were shifting their weight from one foot to another. Meg fell into a disturbed sleep. Humphrey Bogart was peering between wreathes of cigarette smoke at her. Her feet were glued to the spot by great wads of gum. Getting up for the lavatory during the night, she looked out of the window. The shadow was gone from the garden but there was a car parked across the road. A faint glow showed that there was someone smoking in the car. Surely too late for lovers to be smooching.? The clock showed just past four. She climbed back into bed and spent some time trying to escape John Wayne who followed her, six-guns blazing. It was like the shoot out at the OK corral. She woke exhausted to the sound of the bell.

"It's only seven- thirty," she said accusingly as she confronted Sam Piggott. Sergeant Lake was again tucked coyly away behind the trellis. "Must you come so early."

"I don't keep office hours. I work until a job is finished without clock watching. We did wait until morning to be sure you had a good nights sleep." Meg, who felt as though she had had seven minutes dream-free sleep in the last week, made no reply.

"Thank you." They were in the house and shedding their coats before she had time to close the door. "It was a cold night, ground frost everywhere." Meg felt this would hardly trouble you unless you were spending the night outside.

"Was it you watching the house last night?" Her anger was rising again. "Someone was watching me. I can't think why, I'm not going anywhere. Was it you?" she accused the sergeant. It seemed likely that, if such a job were necessary then he, as junior partner, should be given the job. Sergeant Lake was hurt.

"If I'd been watching you lady, you wouldn't have seen me." His professionalism was deeply injured.

"Sometimes a guilty conscience makes us think we are being watched. Don't you agree Mrs. Goodricke?" Sam Piggott was in his 'let's all be good pals' mood. Meg didn't care for it. Almost liked his belligerent accusing tone better.

"What was it you wanted anyway?" Meg was still cross at being disturbed so early.

"What was it? Oh, yes, about the coat." The inspector was smiling, ever so slightly but smiling. "You did say you don't have a green coat?"

"I don't have a green coat," flatly.

"Ah, not now perhaps. But you did have one, did you not?" Why doesn't he get on with it, Meg was more irritated by the minute with this cat and mouse game.

"I do not have and have never had a green coat." It did not sound convincing even to her ears.

"The vicar of your church, Mr. Crabtree is it? He says you have a green coat. And a green hat to match," he added triumphantly.

"I shouldn't think Gilbert Crabtree has the faintest idea about his parishioners' clothing, he barely knows their names." She felt the need to be spiteful and her resentment against the gossipy vicar was rekindled.

"He is quite certain about the coat, as is his sister too."

"Oh, her." Meg's contempt for Grace Crabtree was venomous. "She doesn't know in which way she is pointing."

"The lady is not nearly as vague as people think." Meg made no comment, watching Harry Lake undo another piece of gum and slip it into his mouth. He simultaneously removed the wad already in occupation. It was defly done and obviously the result of much practice. Catching her eye, he grinned sheepishly.

"Chief Inspector Piggott is there a purpose to this visit?"

"Indeed there is," he nodded absently. "I have a green coat in my possession," he waved his hand as though dismissing the idea that he would carry evidence around with him. "A coat that was left at a dry cleaners shop in Chester. A green coat. It was left there by a woman answering to your description. This woman took the coat in with blood stains on it. Told a story about a bad nose bleed." He was patently sceptical on that score.

"I know nothing about it and don't have a green coat." Meg clung to her only defense. The only way out was abject denial. Let the Chief Inspector do what he could he was not able to prove anything. Or was he? Anyway, admit nothing was the advice given by Tudor Baines and by Binny. Meg thought that the solicitor would be asking a fat fee for his advice so it would be a good idea to accept his word. One didn't call the plumber and tell him how to repair the pipe.

"Perhaps you wouldn't mind coming down to the station and taking part in an identification parade? Just to eliminate you from our enquiries, you understand." Meg understood only too well.

"Yes, I would mind and no, I won't be coming to the station."

"Very well. Of course I do not have a warrant to enforce your co-operation. Not just yet." His voice was soft, his smile very fleeting.

Meg showed the two men to the door. Sergeant Lake came sheepishly back for his hat, which he had forgotten. She closed the door and was nearly deafened by the thumping panic rising in her chest.

Chapter 31

ALMOST immediately Meg began her Lady Macbeth routine again. She spent the afternoon cleaning the house, remembering that it had not even been dusted since Binny had acted as fairy God-mother on the day of the funeral. Less than a week but it seemed much longer. She would have started on the garden but it was too sodden after a week of rain. It looked forlorn and bleak and Meg was saddened as she liked gardening. The evening she spent in the same ritualistic pattern, cleaning herself. She varnished her nails, plucked her eyebrows, while listening to her favourite jazz on Charles' player. He had never allowed her to play them, saying they would destroy his needles. Meg knew this was nonsense, the real reason being that he did not like jazz. She pumice stoned her elbows so thoroughly that she winced at the contact of a clean shirt on her raw skin.

Open handed Binny was again prepared to be generous with her time and her dinner. Meg refused reluctantly. She did not want to wear out her welcome there, feeling as she did, that Binny was the only friend she had in the world. There had been no word from Jane, a brief note from Barbara and her husband. Raymond was a member of Charles' golf club and she remembered meeting him once at a club do. It had been quite as boring as she had expected and she had shocked Raymond by not knowing Tom Watson from Jack Nicklaus.

Finally falling into bed, totally exhausted, Meg was convinced that the roar of cannon would not rouse her. She woke in the dark to the sound of rain. Although it was only six she got up and made a pot of coffee. She had often wished she had the ability to enjoy long lie-ins, switching off the world whilst snuggling into the bed clothes. Never having had this ability she felt, once awake, she should be up and face the day. Drinking the coffee she opened the new books and began planning the summer garden. She decided on lots of bright red showy flowers. The kind that Charles said were vulgar. He would go on to explain, as though flowers could be fitted into a circle, the way he relegated people into acceptable or beyond the pale. Meg often wondered if he had classed her as beyond the pale but it was part of his Christian duty to put up with her foibles.

Out of an ill defined sense of grievance she decided to go to church. Gilbert was into another version of his 'love your neighbour as yourself and all will be right with the world. Meg, who felt nothing short of murderous toward most of mankind glowered at Gilbert throughout his sermon. He seemed not a whit affected by her black looks. His sister got up during the communion part of the service but, instead of going to the communion rail, she wandered off and out of the church.

As the congregation was leaving Meg caught a glimpse of Grace wandering about among the graves and engaging in what looked like a long conversation with some of the dead.

Fey was a word that came into Megs' head, she was a little unsure of its meaning but was sure that it summed up the vicars sister admirably. Besides it was more polite than schizophrenia, another word associated with Grace. Gilbert shook her hand warmly and said nothing. Meg wondered what it meant. Gilberts' hand shakes were as rare as summer snow.

Reaching home she decided against a liquid lunch, remembering her half-hearted vow to curb her alcohol consumption and trying to make a real effort. Sitting down picnic style in the living room to chops and green beans, she wondered why she had bothered. She drank her austere glass of orange juice in one swallow, shuddered and coughed at the sharpness. Unbidden recollections of meals shared with Charles came to mind. Sponge puds, treacle tarts, toad in the hole and dumplings. He had very childish tastes in food and a firm believer that you got better value for your money. He would, however, drink quite expensive wine with this schoolish fare. And of course, it was so at variance with his carefully cultivated taste in other things. His Dutch interiors, Japanese prints and choral music, which Meg found thin and insubstantial. Meg sighed at the complexity of human nature. The door bell's peal roused her and she let Binny in with a welcome smile.

Binny nodded approvingly at the remains of the meal and grinned at the orange juice glass. She exclaimed delightedly at the pristine cleanliness of the room and laughed when Meg assured her that the blitz did not just extend to the one room.

Binny said that Meg could have ten out of ten for effort and twelve out of ten for results. She thought this enormously funny and guffawed repeatedly at her humour. Meg realised that the front was up again and the silly-ass Binny was in occupation.

Binny had brought a beautiful azalia as a present, tended in her own greenhouse, she assured Meg, well deserved in view of her diligent housekeeping. Meg gave Binny all Charles' recordings of chamber music. Binny was overwhelmed and Meg explained that it was no sacrifice as she did not care for Charles' choice. In a rush of warmth for Binny Meg put on some of her jazz. The flicker of distaste as Benny Goodman reached a crescendo did not escape Meg and she quickly turned it off and immediately asked about Mr. Micawber.

He was laid low by some doggy virus that gave him a runny nose, sore ears and did dreadful things to his bowels. Binny looked as if her own nose was about to run in sympathy. Meg showed a fascination with every symptom. The door bell sounded, Sam Piggott was on the very top step. Sergeant Lake, one step behind, hat in hand, was chewing rythmically. Meg' tempered flared.

"It's Sunday," she accused.

"I told you I do not take time off until a case is closed." Meg did remember but did not comment.

Binny leapt up and backed hastily into the hall way while acknowledging Megs' introductions.

"Oh, I say," was her comment as Meg opened the door for her.

Chapter 32

RETURNING to the two policemen Meg demanded to know the reason for their visit.

"New developments," the laconic comment caused Sergeant Lake to shift his gaze from Meg and shift his gum to his other cheek. A glower from Sam Piggott silenced him.

"There are new developments but I am not at liberty to disclose them. I will, however, ask if you are prepared to review your statement about Charles Rogerson and your final meeting with him."

Final was stressed ever so slightly but Meg, keyed as she was to an intake of breath, did not miss it.

"I've told you all I can." The door bell sounded again. Tudor Baines stumbled headlong into the room.

"Superintendent." He had obviously met the policeman before.

"Chief Inspector." Corrected Sam Piggott. "A social call Mr. Baines?" There was no effort made to shake hands and the solicitor was busy cleaning his by the friction method.

"No, indeed. My client asked me to call and advise her." To Megs astonishment he winked at her. Of course, Binny must have rung him, firm in the conviction that Meg was on her way to the gallows at that very moment.

"Mr. Baines we have firm evidence that Mrs. Goodricke was present when Charles Rogerson died suddenly. Suddenly and violently," he added for good measure.

"And the nature of this evidence?"

"We have identified a coat belonging to Mrs. Goodricke which has Charles Rogersons' blood on it."

"How can you know it's this man's blood?"

"We know his blood type and it matches that on the coat. We do know that the coat is hers."

"Perhaps. But as to whether the blood is that of the dead man, you surely cannot be certain of that? There must be people of the same type. Unless it is extremely rare? Even then it would not be unique I think."

"It was group AB and that is rare enough."

"Unusual perhaps, but certainly not unheard of. I wouldn't say rare Chief Inspector. Something like five percent of the population belong to this group if I remember correctly" His knowledge of forensic matters was no surprise to Meg. She felt she had never known Tudor Baines. "I can't agree that this has anything to do with my client. The evidence is purely circumstantial. You will have to do better than this Chief Inspector. Much better." He was like a school master chiding a lazy pupil.

"I will. I'll do much better." Sam Piggott responded in like manner as though assuring the solicitor that he would spend more time on his prep in future.

"The coat is Mrs. Goodricke's though. We have established that."

"Did you give the coat away at any time? Send it to the jumble sale perhaps?" Tudor Baines looked appealingly at

Meg willing her to enter into the conspiracy with him. Sam Piggott was not going to let him get away with that one.

"The coat is new Mr. Baines, it's hardly likely she would give away a new coat is it?"

"She may not have cared for the colour after all. Women do make impulse buys and then decide they have made the wrong decision. My wife does. She has dozens of pairs of shoes which I know she never wears and then goes and buys more. Many, many more." Meg had a mental image of Tudor Baines locking up his wife to keep her out of the shoe shops and his wife gleefully smuggling shoes in the house disguised in grocery bags. She giggled and all three men turned to her with various expressions of amazement.

"That is beside the point, Mrs. Goodricke is unable to explain the blood stains down the front of her coat. It's not her blood." Sam was quick with this addition as he saw Tudor Baines open his mouth. "We have checked her records at the hospital and she is group 'o'. We thought she might have been a patient at the Infirmary at Waster-burn at some time. Most people are. And of course you have been, haven't you Mrs Goodricke?"

Meg gazed blankly at the Chief Inspector. She had no recollection of ever being at the hospital.

"It is some years ago, but they never destroy their records. Thousands of them they have. Everyone who has ever passed through their doors I think." Meg remembered. Charles had taken her, early in their marriage, to the Infirmary referred by old Mr. Hornby, the dentist they shared. He felt Meg needed more specialist care than he was able to give and she had gone as a day patient to have wisdom teeth removed.

It had been a rather bloody operation but she had not needed the blood for which she had been cross-matched. It had only been a precaution as they thought she might be a bleeder. Not a true haemophiliac but someone who bled excessively. Often linked with her hair colouring the surgeon reassured her.

"Those records must surely be private?" Tudor Baines sounded deeply shocked.

"Perhaps you gave your permission?" A questioning look at Meg. She shook her head. "Then of course you had a warrant from a magistrate?" This with a keen look at Sam Piggott. The inspectors face was blank. "Without permission your methods must have been unscrupulous and certainly not admissible in any court." Harry Lake sniggered and was again on the receiving end of Sams' most withering stare.

"So if the blood isn't Mrs. Goodricke's and not necessarily Charles Rogersons, then whose is it?" Sam Piggotts terrier methods were establishing themselves.

"The kiddie in the park!" Megs voice came out louder than she intended and the solicitor started visibly.

"You really have no need to say anything." The words were a suggestion, the tone a command from Tudor.

"I had forgotten about the little boy in the park." She was gabbling as she elaborated

"No need at all." the warning went unheeded again as she prattled on, always at her most colourful and inventive under stress.

Chapter 33

Meg was irrepressible. She went into great detail about a child who had fallen off the slide and cut his leg on a skate he had left at the bottom. There was no end to her inventiveness once she was launched.

"I picked him up and he bled a lot. I clutched him to me." Meg, who had never been within touching distance of a child, could see the scene in her head.

"What was he called?" Sam Piggott had no romantic streak in him. His was a cruel world of facts, times, dates and names. Meg almost felt sorry for someone so shut off from the niceties of life.

"Called? I haven't the faintest idea. He was just a child. A child in need of help." Sam Piggott looked as though stray children, forgotten and nameless were outside his experience. He looked as though he didn't believe in Megs' urchin.

"What sort of age might he have been Mrs. Goodricke?"

"I really don't know." She tried to look as if she had never been a child. "He had fair hair and blue eyes."

"So, have thousands of children." The inspector sounded cross. Harry Lake silenced another snigger by posting more gum in his mouth. Tudor Baines looked as if he would like something to bite on.

"Did you take him to the hospital?

"Goodness, no. You can't take strange children away with you." Meg felt he should be more conversant with the law. "His mother may have taken him," she added helpfully.

"I suppose we could go through all the casualty records to see if she did." Harry Lake blenched at this. He saw such a job coming his way.

"I don't suppose she took the coat to the dry cleaners for you?"

"She was much too busy with the boy. I took it myself." Tudor Baines sighed and gave a slight shrug of his narrow shoulders.

"I do think, Inspector Piggott, that until you have some concrete evidence that you really should stop badgering my client like this,"

"Chief Inspector," corrected the sergeant. He was like one of those Kelly men toys. The little fat men who bounce up as soon as they are knocked down. Sam Piggott shrugged on his coat with a face like thunder. He waited at the door for his sergeant to catch up and looked as though he would like to ram Harry's gum far down his throat. His farewell tone he tried to make as menacing as possible.

"I shall be back." Tudor Baines at last came into his own.

"I would consider it a courtesy if you would let me know when further interviews are to take place." No response. The solicitor moved across to the big armchair which Meg still thought of as Charles' chair. He had a notebook on his knee, biro at the ready. He looked up but did not respond to Megs' smile.

"Miss Parsons rang and said you needed help. This I'm quite ready to give but I must insist first that we have the whole truth out into the open. There must be no secrets between us. No secrets. If I am to help I must know everything. We can take it as read that you did know Charles Rogerson. I think that you were with him when he died. I need to know if you killed him."

"No, I had nothing to do with it." She saw him close his notebook and begin to scrabble his pen into his pocket. The realisation of how utterly alone she would be when facing the police accusations came to her. Meg had never really believed in police brutality; had thought they were inventions of scaremongers. The idea of truncheons and fists in kidneys were silly. She did realise though that there were more subtle ways of intimidating a suspect or prisoner. Meg suddenly slumped into the other armchair, legs splayed inelegantly, arms between her knees gazing at the carpet dejectedly. Carefully lifting the big armchair Tudor Baines came and sat in front of Meg, knee to knee.

"Tell me." Raising weary eyes and leaden shoulders Meg looked into his button-black eyes.

"Alright. I did know Charles Rogerson. I was with him when he died, it was his blood on my coat. But," she spat fiercely, "I did not kill him." She was aware of the solicitor letting his breath out slowly and audibly. His lungs finally emptied.

"I thought so," was his only comment.

"It was an accident," once launched there was no stopping Meg. She took a deep breath. "He was on one side of the room and I was on the other. I could not have possibly made him fall on the bacon slicer. It was carelessness on his part. He fell straight onto the machine, gave a gurgle and within a few moments he was dead."

"Not quite just like that surely. I must have more detail." He poked his ear diligently with his biro pen.

"That was it," Megs' finger snapped. "It was over in no time. Death must have been instantaneous," she diagnosed.

Tudor Baines leapt up and stood behind the chair. This is the bacon machine," he plumped up a cushion and placed it on the back of the chair. "Where is the step?" He handed her a book.

"Just here," Meg placed it on the edge of the fireside rug.

"And you were standing where?"

"A good distance away, about here." Meg positioned herself in the bay of the window and tried to look distant.

"I will accept your word. What happened then?" He sounded cross with himself.

"He bled to death." Meg found this simple statement most dramatic.

"Not an instantaneous death then. Did he say anything?"

"Goodness no. He gave a sort of gurgle and by the time I had made it round the counter, to see of I could help," she added virtuously, "He was gone, very pale with staring eyes."

"A shock for you."

"A terrible shock. I didn't know what to do for a moment. I was paralysed with indecision." It was a ringing phrase and she repeated it to be sure he appreciated the full drama of it all.

Chapter 34

TUDOR Baines was not slow with his cues.

"I can see you standing there in an agony of indecision, gazing horror struck at the dead body. Did you kneel down and touch the body and thus got blood on your coat?"

"Oh, no. the blood splashed on me when he fell." She realised her mistake too late.

"But you were on the other side of the room, at least three metres away." he said measuring the distance from chair to window with his eager eye.

"Well, blood does go a long way when an artery is severed. It was like a fountain."

"Quite. What did you do then, when you had recovered from the shock?"

"I shall never recover from the shock." Her tone was reproachful. "I dropped the latch on the shop door and went home. There was nothing I could do for Charles. There was no reason to get involved. It wasn't my fault and I didn't know him very well. I couldn't help by getting involved."

"You were already involved dear lady. Deeply, deeply involved. How long had you known the man?"

"That day was the first time I had met him." Tudor Baines' eyebrows danced up and down his forehead in agitation.

"And you went to his house, having just met him?"

"Well, it was to his shop. I had no intention of going to his flat above the shop." The need to whiten herself rose urgently.

"That diary the police have is a load of old rubbish. Charles Rogerson must just have made up the things he wrote. They certainly weren't the truth."

"A diary?"

"Yes, didn't you know about it? Chief Inspector Piggott told me there was a diary about an affair I was having with Charles or Chuck I think he was known as. It's not true Mr. Baines. I hardly knew the man and certainly not as well as the inspector says. I'm sure he did not believe me when I said the diary was just fantasy. People have no right to make up stories like that." Tudor smiled blandly at Meg.

"Unfortunately, there are such people. What other evidence have the police got against you? Letters perhaps? Photographs? Any other means of linking you to him?"

"None there can't be any evidence because I did not know him." Her voice had reached crescendo pitch.

"Be calm, dear lady, be calm. I think I should go and see the Chief Inspector and find which way the land lies."

"You don't think I'm in any danger do you, Mr. Baines?" Meg tried to make her tone casual, a little disinterested. The fluttering in her chest became a thunderous pounding as he spoke. He chose his words very carefully.

" As to that, I do not know. Certainly, you are in a very serious position. Sam Piggott is a persistent man. He will not let go until he has established the truth. One way or another," he added menacingly.

A pint of coffee and several cigarettes later Meg began to brighten, remembering her appointment with Sven she began to plan her clothing for the day. Finally deciding that slacks and a heavy sweater would be most suitable, she went about the household chores with a better heart.

By mid-day she was looking forward to an afternoon with Sven. She hoped that today she would be able to break through the superman front of Sven's pose as athlete of the year and make him responsive in the way of other men she had met. Surely the same hormones and adrenalin coursed through his veins. Like most other men she thought, remembering Gilbert Crabtree and Gordon.

After the frequent visits of Sam Piggott over the last few days Meg began to feel uneasy about the policeman. It was ridiculous, after her many complaints of hounding, to feel neglected when they did not call to see her. The doorbell was silent, the telephone stilled throughout the morning.

Setting out for her meeting, she looked up and down the road. A neighbour, innocently waxing his car, was treated to a very hard stare.

Sven was waiting outside the Linden Tree. His happy grin cheered Meg and they set out, in his car, for Wasterbum and the skating rink.

Sven was dressed in a very tight track suit which showed off every tempting bulge. His conversation, light and frivolous, was just what Meg needed after the intense concentration needed to keep up with Sam Piggott.

The rink was indeed quiet as Sven had promised. There was an elderly couple skating exquisitely to some unheard waltz music of their own. Meg was shy of making a fool of herself when she saw the waltzing couple. Sven had quickly laced up his boots and glided smoothly onto the ice. He did a graceful turn of the rink and then came across to help Meg with the hired boots. Laughing, he pulled her to her feet and held her close. Lovely, she thought, so far so good. Meg's feet went persistently in opposite directions. Sven allowed her to drop to the ice a couple of times when her uncoordinated feet would not obey her. She felt the cold of the ice through her slacks when she fell but the comfort of his arms was worth the minor discomfort. His arm went under hers and cupped her breast. Meg gasped and leaned more firmly into him. He seemed not to notice her co-operation and moved the hand to tuck it round her waist. Sven chuckled and skated off, leaving Meg stranded and foolish in the middle of the rink, afraid to move. In answer to her pleas and pathetic wobbling, he came to rescue her. He murmured something, she pulled his head nearer to hear him. She looked over his blonde head. Her eyes gazed straight into those of Chief Inspector Piggott.

Chapter 35

HARRY Lake, standing some way behind his superior, grinned broadly at Meg. She did not respond. The Chief Inspector raised his hand and gestured to Meg, indicating that she was to come off the ice and across to him. Lemming-like Meg made her way to the beckoning hand. A sure and certain knowledge of impending doom oppressed her. The joy had gone from the day.

Sam Piggott helped Meg off the ice and placed a chair for her. He said nothing. Surprisingly Harry Lake bent down and unlaced the skates. He did not speak either but went off to the rink office bearing the boots before him, wary of the sharp edges. He returned carrying Meg's shoes but these were clutched to him. Slipping her shoes on, Meg looked up expectantly. Sam Piggott cleared his throat.

"Margaret Elizabeth Goodricke I am arresting you for the murder of Charles Arthur Rogerson. You are not obliged to say anything but whatever you do say may be taken down and given in evidence."

Sergeant Lake stood, notebook in hand, pencil at the ready, to record any comments Meg might choose to make. She had nothing to say, her contempt for these men was profound. How could they link her name with that of a seedy grocer who had virtually killed himself through his own carelessness.

The Chief Inspector continued in his formal and distant approach. He escorted her outside and handed her carefully into the police car. Looking around Meg saw that the sergeant was talking to Sven and making the occasional entry in his notebook. He nodded curtly at Sven and walked quickly to the car.

"My car," protested Meg. "It's in the car park in the market square in Sandford. Can't I go and pick it up?" She realised her plea carried no conviction.

"We have made arrangements for your car to be removed," said Sam Piggott stiffly. Arrangements? How could they have made arrangements. How did they know where her car was?

"How do you know where my car is?"

"We saw you put it there." So, they had not forgotten about her this morning. They had been very much aware of all her doings. Had probably watched her meeting Sven and so followed her to Wasterburn.

"The man I was with, he knows nothing of all this. He's just a casual friend," she added lamely.

"We are well aware of Mr. Svensson's involvement." Mr. Svensson? Sven Svensson? She could not credit the implausibility of such a name.

"We know where to contact him, should the need arise." Meg looked at this new Sam Piggott. No longer the friendly father figure he was cool and distant in a way she found very sinister and uncomfortable.

Harry Lake drove the car back to Castlebridge at great speed. They stopped at the police station and almost immediately a woman police constable got in the front with Harry. Meg saw in the driving mirror he gave her a broad wink. Sam introduced her as Police Constable Dodd. The officer flashed a mechanical smile at Meg and then turned to look straight ahead.

The car turned into Meg's road and pulled up outside her house. As he helped her from the car the Chief Inspector held her hand for a moment.

"Constable Dodd will go with you Mrs. Goodricke. I would like you to pack a small case with such clothing as you might need for a few days." Meg could find nothing to say. She went upstairs, closely followed by the officer. Standing in the bedroom she was unable to do anything for herself and allowed the constable to suggest things. Meg watched while the things were packed in a weekend grip. Meg recognised this with a jolt as being from Charles' university days. The policewoman allowed Meg to slip off her trousers; which were wet on the seat from her tumble on the ice; and put on a skirt. She watched with disinterest as Meg changed her underwear which was also damp. At last they were ready and came downstairs, the police officer carrying her case. The two men rose as one. Harry held out his hand for the case, Sam opened the door and Meg found herself being handed into the police car once more. This time she was seated between the police woman and the inspector. I'm like the cheese in a sandwich she thought and giggled. Three pairs of eyes turned to stare in astonishment.

"We are going to Chester Police Headquarters, where I am stationed you will remember," explained the Chief Inspector. "There you will be formally charged again, examined by the police surgeon and then remanded in custody overnight. You will be brought before the magistrates in the morning, You may have a solicitor with you."

Although the inspector made this seem a good idea Meg did not think the sight of Tudor Baines would bring joy to anyone's heart.

"I haven't done anything," she said sulkily and settling back in the car, she closed her eyes and said nothing during the drive to Chester.

The police headquarters were confusing. There were many uniformed officers going purposefully about. There were seats in the reception area. These were occupied by a very dirty man whose bare feet were tucked under his chair and a woman sitting with two teenage girls. Flotsam and jetsam thought Meg and giggled again.

Meg was escorted past the reception and shown into a large, sparsely furnished room. There was a table, badly scuffed and decorated with overflowing ash trays and three wooden chairs. A telephone hung on the wall next to a poster advising where the nearest venereal diseases clinic was to be found. Harry Lake pulled out a chair for Meg so that she was seated back to the poster and facing the door. Sam Piggott came bustling in with a sheaf of papers under his arm. Policewoman Dodd sidled in behind him and went across to perch on the window sill. From there she appeared to take no further notice of the proceedings but stared out at the traffic. Harry Lake left the room when the others came in. His jaw had ceased the rhythmic chomping and Meg wondered if he had gone to replace his chewing gum stock. She was surprised to see the inspector uncap a fountain pen. He squared off the corners of his papers, tapped them into a neat pile and placed his pen across them. It was all very meticulous.

"Do you smoke?"

"Sometimes, when I'm worried," she mumbled.

"You may smoke now if you wish." He moved the full and dirty ashtrays to the end of the table and produced a clean one from a drawer. He set this in front of Meg and produced a packet of cigarettes and a Ronson lighter. "Please," he invited. Meg ignored him.

"We are now in a position to proceed with the case for the prosecution. There ..." His voice droned on, and Meg stopped listening. The enormity of her position was just coming home to her. She still found it incredible. Her belief in the legal system was that, if you were innocent, you had nothing to fear. Meg looked upon herself as totally innocent. She was nevertheless very fearful. Perhaps it was Nemesis, a retribution for killing off her husband. Poor Charles, sentimentally, he wasn't too bad really. Sometimes.

Megs' wool gathering was interrupted by the door being flung open and Harry Lake appearing balancing a tea tray shoulder high. Depositing it on the table Harry handed a cup to each of them, taking one for himself and sitting in the other chair. Only Officer Dodd thanked him. He tipped back his chair so that it rested on it's two rear legs. This made it possible for him to slip his fingers in the pocket of his too-tight trousers. He unwrapped the chocolate bar he had wriggled out and started munching noisily. Sam Piggott shot him a look of total venom. Sam waited until Harry had licked his fingers and wiped them on his trousers.

"So, you see Mrs. Goodricke, you are in a very serious position."

"Very dodgy," the sergeant was barely intelligible through his chocolate.

"What do I have to say to convince you that you are wrong?" Meg did not sound convincing even to herself.

"The evidence is irrefutable," murmured the inspector. This was just the expression used all those years ago when the twelve year old Meg had stood defiant and sulky in the headmistress' study and denied that she had stolen money from other pupil's coat pockets. She stared into Sam Piggotts' face and tried to capture again that defiant childhood attitude. She failed miserably and felt very small and vulnerable. The inspector spoke quietly to the policewoman and Meg found the other woman's elbow under her own and she was being shepherded out and back to the stark room with the antiseptic smell and the narrow bed.

The day seemed to telescope. No sooner had a young officer removed the meal of cold meat and tomato which she had refused to eat, than he was bringing a milk drink and sweet biscuits.

Meg had a vague recollection of a tall man, with a ridiculous goatee beard, introducing himself as Doctor Carstairs the police surgeon. She had passively submitted to the stethoscope on her chest, the ophthalmoscope in her eyes and the silly hammer tapping below her knees and at her elbows. He had asked questions about her uneventful medical history. He nodded several times and then asked if she had ever seen a psychiatrist. The doctor made it sound as though they were a rare breed one paid to see in an animal compound. Meg murmured that she had seen one on a couple of occasions as a child. The school had referred her to the local Child Guidance Centre after the missing dinner money episode.

Meg had fond memories of the large-bosomed, motherly psychiatrist. She had listened attentively to Megs' stories about her father. Meg had explained that, although he officially worked for the Light and Marine Insurance Company, he was really a deep sea diver who worked at night. He would launch a row boat and dive from the rocks near the harbour entrance. Their house, little Meg assured the doctor, was filled with treasures from the bottom of the sea. Lost from Spanish galleons. The station sergeant brought a short, dapper man into the room and introduced him as Doctor Turgel. The little man bowed from the neck and clicked hi heels together. Meg had tried not to laugh at this unusual behaviour. From this and the faint accent she assumed him to be German.

Doctor Turgel stayed about an hour. Much of this time was taken up with long silences. Meg did not feel discomforted by these. Doctor Turgel would ask a question to which she would reply. Not honestly of course, that was not her way, but politely and informatively enough. Many of the silences had followed her replies. Perhaps he is waiting for me to elaborate she surmised. She did not feel the need to do so. He sat quietly contemplating her. Mostly he studied the top of her head when she dropped it and studied the fingers in her lap. Meg's covert glances had revealed his habit of pulling his left ear with his right hand. Occasionally he varied this by pulling the opposite ear with the other hand. Meg found this fascinating. No wonder he has such big ears she thought and giggled.

Chapter 36

DOCTOR Turgel jumped from topic to topic, his questions very random. From her childhood to her marriage. From her parents to her adolescence. Meg found it difficult changing tack in this way. One time she wondered if she had slipped up and told contradictory accounts of her youth. She was reassured when the doctor did not challenge her on this.

About Charles' death she was brief to the point of being terse. She agreed it was a rather premature death for someone in previous good health. She did point out that heart disease was affecting much younger men. Yes, she was comfortable financially. No, she had not hated her mother. Yes, she thought she had been a happy child. Yes, her father was a mild, agreeable man who never raised his voice. No, she had never had a pet animal as a child.

The questions seemed pointless, her answers became monosyllabic as she became more bored. She was not sorry when the little man got up, clicked his heels and bowed stiffly, chin on his chest. He opened the door very wide as though he were a big man needing a roomy exit and closed it with exaggerated softness. Another policewoman appeared. She took Meg to a wash room, miraculously produced Meg's sponge bag and nightclothes. Meg spit paste viciously into the basin. She answered Meg's query in a bored voice and informed her that officer Dodd had gone of duty and that she was there on night duty. She did not offer her name and shrugged when asked where was the cord from the dressing gown.

Meg spent the night wishing someone would turn out the light and trying to persuade herself that the hard bed and thin pillow were good for her spine. The next morning was cold. Rain coursed down the grimy window of the antiseptic room. There was an intrusive smell of fried food. Doors were banged, heavy feet stomped up long flights of stairs. There was the sound of many loud voices. She assumed they matched the heavy feet.

Meg sat on the edge of the narrow bed and dared herself to set foot on the cold lino, barren of any carpet or rug. Policewoman Dodd appeared while Meg sat there. She was cheerful, gave a gloomy weather report and asked Meg if she had slept. The previous ritual of Megs' clothes appearing was repeated. Breakfast was brought by a young constable who leered at his colleague and was ignored. The meal was also ignored apart from the cup of tea from which Meg drank deeply. A cleaner came and pushed a mop around the floor. Two constables came and stripped the bed and made it up with fresh sheets.

There were some magazines on the chair and Meg picked them up as a means of shutting out the boring comments of the policewoman. The problem page, which was where she always began her reading of such publications, was tucked away among the deodorant adverts. She was never to know the answer to 'Desperate of York' as one of the cadets threw open the door and announced with great pride, "Your solicitor ma'am." Tudor Baines looked windswept. He pushed his hair wrong way across his parting and held out his hand.

"Oh, dear lady, what a tangled web we weave, what a tangled web."

"I haven't practiced to deceive," said Meg capping his quotation.

"Come," without waiting for an answer or waiting to see of she followed, Tudor Baines left the room. Meg found herself almost trotting to keep abreast of him. He swept into the interview room she had occupied the previous day. It was cleaner this time. Sitting in her chair of yesterday Meg had an overwhelming sense of deja-vu.

"I have the depositions which were sent to the Director of Public Prosecutions," he began without preamble. He had his brief-case open, papers out on the table and was rifling through them before Meg had settled in her chair.

"The case they have against you is black very black indeed."

"You told me that the other day," Meg was sullen and took no pains to hide it.

"Quite. But if you had told me the truth in the first place, or would tell it now...." Meg said nothing. "However, a little light in the tunnel. I have been to see Caroline Francis." This raised eyebrows from Meg and he carried on. "Caroline Francis is formerly Caroline Rogerson sister of Charles Rogerson."

He looked as though awaiting applause.

"So? What does it matter?"

"This lady knew her brother better than anyone and she says that Chuck, as she called him, was always good at telling fairy stories. He would romanticise any and every situation and lie about anything and everything. She said it was quite possible that Chuck had made up the diary entries, making a story out of nothing."

"I told you how it was but you didn't believe me."

"This does put a slightly different complexion on things in that it might show you in a better light. Not as wicked as it was first thought." The solicitor addressed no-one in particular, seemed to expect no answer.

"What happens next?" Fearful of his reply Meg hung her head and pulled her fingers apart until they cracked sickeningly.

"A court appearance, a remand and bail I hope. Appearance at the Crown Court eventually". The address was spine chilling.

"What can they do to me?" The role of helpless victim did not impress.

"Leave it in my hands." He spread his fingers as though to show that this was the most reliable place for ones' troubles.

Chapter 37

THE next hour was the most horrible of her life. She sat for what seemed an age in a long tiled corridor, a policeman and policewoman Dodd either side of her. When she tried to shuffle her chair away from the officer's cheap aftershave, she found that the chair was fastened to the floor.

Meg heard a man shouting her name in full as though she were lost and he seeking to find her. The officers led her into a panelled room. There were three people, two men and a woman, sitting behind a polished table. Meg was sat-at a smaller table facing the three. There was an island of highly buffed floor between them. The police officers disappeared and magically Tudor Baines was seated beside Meg. Where he had been during the long corridor wait she could not surmise.

A man stood and pulled a gown around him, it was like a graduate's gown. Charles had one in his wardrobe, momento of his university days. Meg wondered why this man wore such a gown.

"Margaret Elizabeth Goodricke." intoned the clerk and Tudor Baines scrambled Meg to her feet and stood beside her. His arm was under her elbow, his fingers nipping her funny bone. She did not find it funny. "You are charged" the voice went on and Meg tried to shut it out. The occasional word slipped through 'murder', the most noticable one was like a sudden blow across her head, 'but' she began at one point. Tudor gripped her arm so tightly that the pain drove the protest away. She was in the corridor again a few moments later.

"What happened?" She turned to Tudor Baines as though he were the interpreter of a foreign language.

"The magistrates have remanded you. Unfortunately, they would not hear of bail. They have remanded you in custody for social and psychiatric reports. The Crown appearance will be in about six weeks. If we're lucky," he added savagely.

"Does that mean I can't go home?" Meg was truly appalled at the turn events had taken. "Can't go home for SIX WEEKS?"

"That's about it," drily. Meg sat down with a thump on one of the nailed- down chairs.

"Oh, God."

"I could ask your priest to visit." Did Tudor see Gilbert Crabtree as a substitute for God or was the association mere chance?

"Gilbert Crabtree is a friend is he not?" Meg laughed a high, hysterical laugh. She was taken back to the room with a bed and a blank view.

"Just temporary, until we can make arrangements," explained the policeman. Arrangements about what? Things were slipping away from Meg in a manner that was foreign to her. She, who had always been captain of her own destiny, was having to give herself up into the hands of strangers and do their bidding like a small child. It was frightening.

Meg sat on the edge of the bed and sipped at the contents of the enamel mug which a young constable had brought. She surmised the contents were coffee, it was difficult to tell. Tudor Baines appeared before the mug was drained to the depths. His hand rubbing was more vigorous than ever. He had a hurried air of embarrassment about him. His voice was hearty and loud.

"The best thing dear lady, much the best thing. Proper care and assessment. Save a lot of time and hassle. Best thing all round."

"Tudor," her tone was bordering on stride. Inside she felt a hard knot in her solar plexus twist and turn. Trying to moderate her tone, she looked deep into his button-black eyes. "Tudor what are you talking about? What would be for the best?" He lifted his eyes to a spot beyond her left shoulder.

"The magistrates have advised that you be remanded to the prison hospital, the psychiatric wing," he mumbled.

"They certainly made up their minds about me." Meg was more angry than she had ever been. "Do they think I don't know what's going on? I do not need psychiatric help. Just a good solicitor," she added bitterly.

Tudor had been gone only a few minutes when Officer Dodd arrived carrying Meg's overcoat. Her conversation was bright, cheerful and empty as she led Meg out of the building. A police sergeant sat in the back seat and he moved a box file so that Meg could sit beside him.

"Where are we going?" asked Meg bleakly.

"Not far," his voice was a soft lilting Welsh. "It's only about fifteen miles to the hospital."

"Which hospital?" Meg thought should know it but it was far from her home town.

"Saint Jude's", was the soft answer. Where else thought Meg. Where else would I go but somewhere whose saint was the patron of lost causes.

Chapter 38

THE building was long and low. The next few weeks seemed very long and she certainly felt low.

Doctor Turgel, or Hans, as he insisted Meg call him, visited her five or six times in the first couple of weeks. Each time he stayed perhaps an hour and again much of the time was taken up with long silences.

Some time during the second week a young girl came in and introduced herself as Abigail Bush. She wore jeans and training shoes. Her cotton t-shirt had C.N.D. printed across it. The conversation with Abigail was brief. They discussed the weather, the local by- elections. They tutted over a recent disaster in Spain in which some people had died and enthused over a town in Portugal. They had both enjoyed a holiday there. They shook hands, the girl hoisted her tote bag onto her thin shoulder and they parted with smiles.

Tudor Baines was most interested in this visit and explained to Meg that Abigail was a psychiatrist appointed by the prosecution to assess Meg's condition.

"Condition, what condition?" protested Meg. She felt things swimming away again.

"She was trying to judge your mental state and your suitability to stand trial."

"But I didn't tell her anything," protested Meg.

"Just so, just so. She will no doubt say that you are entirely sane," said Tudor bitterly when Meg gave him an account of their meeting.

"But I am, it's true."

"Hmm, just so, just so."

"You don't seem very pleased."

"I am not displeased," he said carefully. "It really is a question of presenting things in a way that should be in your best interests."

"How can Abigail Bush be against me?"

"She can present the facts as she sees them. Perhaps differently to the way we want them to be seen. There is a vast difference between someone who is sane and deliberately sets out to murder and a person who is offering a plea of manslaughter due to diminished responsibility."

"What kind of difference?"

"A capital murder charge carries a sentence of life imprisonment. A diminished responsibility means you would be offered help and would be sent to a hospital rather than prison." Meg was inexperienced in this field and was unable to see that a life sentence in prison would mean perhaps serving six or eight years. A referral to a hospital for the criminally insane would mean a term of years decided at the discretion of the doctors. An indeterminate sentence.

"What we are trying to do is present a plea in your favour. I really think it best that we plead diminished responsibility.

"Say I'm too potty to know what's going on?"

"Not at all dear lady. Not at all. Hans Turgel and Gilbert Crabtree and myself we all feel it would be in your best interests to have you sent to a hospital rather than prison."

"They are really tempting alternatives," Meg was scathing. "Are there no other options?"

"Not worth considering, not really."

"How about I DIDN'T DO IT?"

"Oh, come now, come now, come." Tudor Baines excelled himself.

"But what reasons have they got for saying I need psychiatric help?"

"The reports are rather long and wordy. Passing mention to psychopathy or sociopathy. References to inappropriate affect and lack of empathy for others all of which might support such findings. However, no definite diagnosis has been made. Much more extensive and deeper studies are needed."

"So I'm to become their lab rat while they tinker with my innermost feelings!"

"It would not be quite like that and you would be well looked after."

"I don't need looking after. I need to go home." The sheer frustration of trying to get all the other members of officialdom to see her view and failing, finally reduced Meg to the inevitable tears. The solicitor refused to be impressed by the torrent of self pity and waited quietly for the storm to pass.

"Oh. Piss off", she shouted at his already retreating back.

"I hear you had a fall out with your solicitor," said

Hans Turgel, smoothly dropping the remark into the conversation.

"He takes too much upon himself." Meg was too angry to be surly on this day. "He has obviously been talking to Gilbert. By what right? What does Gilbert Crabtree know anyway?"

"He is a very sincere man who has your interests at heart."

"Do you know him too?"

"I have spoken to him, yes. He does know a lot about you. Much of it from your husband."

"Charles?" her astonishment was genuine.

"I understand they were great friends."

"That's true, they were two of a kind." Despite being pressed Meg refused to elaborate on this statement.

Chapter 39

GILBERT had visited one afternoon. He brought greetings from some of the neighbours. Mostly they were casual acquaintances from Charles' golf club, or people who attended the church. No doubt they were enjoying the sensationalism. Gilbert reported that his sister was praying for Meg. This revelation failed to uplift. Binny Parsons, he said when Meg pressed him, was busy doing work for the meals-on-wheels services. Gilbert had brought a small case with him and explained that the police had allowed him access to her house and he had brought her some clothes. He told Meg that the money for the car had been paid into her account. They agreed that the car was well looked after. Charles had vacuumed, washed and polished until it shone like a good deed in a naughty world. Throughout the visit he side stepped any reference to his friendship with Charles which Tudor Baines had mentioned. Gilbert admitted he missed Charles but went no further with that remark. He seemed relieved when the meeting came to an end and Meg wondered if the visit had been to re-assure her that the car money was deposited. But bringing the clothes had been a kind thought. It was toward the end of one of Hans Turgel's silent interviews that Meg mentioned her father. They had been talking about what Meg might have done with her life had she taken a different path. She mentioned that she would have gone to sea and made the navy her career. It was then that she had mentioned her father, who was a chronic messer-about in boats.

The mention of her father was a sudden ray of light to the doctor. He brightened visibly and sat up straight. His usual laid back attitude was gone.

"Tell me about your father." It was almost a command.

"He was a lovely man, he thought the world of me. Unlike my mother," she added bitterly. "She didn't like me at all."

"I'm sure that's not so."

"But it is! She resented the relationship I had with my father."

"Are you sure you did not resent the relationship they had with each other?"

"No, it wasn't like that, it was different. My father would do anything for me." Meg was aware of the brown eyes looking over the top of his glasses. She immediately felt she had to justify herself.

"Mother was jealous because she could not go sailing with him. She was always sea-sick. So it was father and me together." Meg had always refused to acknowledge that her mother had been able to see right through Meg. She was never a victim of her daughter's craftiness.

"You were able to manipulate your father." It was a statement and as such quite unusual for the doctor, who never passed judgement or opinion on any topic.

"No, he did things for me, gave me what I wanted because he loved me. He was a soft, gentle man. I miss him very much." Her bottom lip trembled appealingly. Hans Turgel, like Tudor Baines, was unimpressed.

The psychiatrist looked coldly at Meg.

"He was a weak man who could be manipulated and twisted by a scheming litle girl who later became a calculating young woman." Meg gazed at him with tear-filled eyes.

"It wasn't like that, you are wrong."

"What was it like then? I think you married Charles thinking him a soft man, like your father. A man you thought you could manipulate and who would give you all your own way. You were disappointed and frustrated when you discovered he had more character that you had estimated."

It was a long speech for the little doctor and Meg was more astonished because it was so unexpected. But she was not to be let off so lightly.

"I think your husband knew you very well and, being a loyal man, he felt he had to stick by you. However, being also human, he had to confide his troubles and fears to someone. This is why Gilbert Crabtree knows you so well. He knows you at secondhand from Charles." Meg gasped and stumbled to her feet.

"I hate you!" she spat.

"That is quite usual in these circumstances. You are projecting your feelings. Perhaps you see your mother in me. She saw through you I expect." Meg was never one to accept the truth. She refused it now although she knew it for what it was.

Meg saw that the infuriating little man had more to offer. She felt unable to get up and walk away. She sat feeling like a mouse waiting to be pounced on by the stalking cat.

"I think you realised that Charles could not be manipulated in the way you wanted, that he knew you too well to allow you to crush him. I think that is when you decided to look for other men. Not necessarily for a sexual relationship. That was only part of the possessive process. Another tool in the game. The only surprise to me is that it should be slightly twisted. Perhaps it was the dead grocer having the same name as your husband. If it weren't for that I would not have expected you to kill him. I would have thought, without a doubt, that you would have killed your husband Charles.

Also by the same author

CATHOLIC CUCKOOS

Naïve Lewis meets knowledgeable Angela. To his surprise they are very quickly married. Several babies are born before Lewis begins to suspect that they are not all his children.

He goes to Ireland in pursuit of the father of some of his family and meets Bernadette, a woman who is desperate for a baby.

Sometime after he returns home Bernadette arrives on his doorstep. The baby she is expecting is going to be related to his family, although not his child.

Angela welcomes Bernadette into their home, where she lives until the lure of other men means that she leaves.

Available from www.ypdbooks.com